My dear Rose,

On the Planet of Music, I met two kindred spirits who loved each other despite their differences. I realized that there's no limit to what love can accomplish. Every day I'm learning a little more about the grown-up world—and about myself.

How would I react if you or Fox were in danger? Would I be able to think clearly, or would my feelings force me down the Snake's path? I hope I never have to choose between you or Fox and what's best for the universe—but the Snake keeps trying to find a way to make me choose. Why? What's his goal?

I'll try to learn more now that we're approaching a new planet, this time with a lush forest.

Is the Snake really there?

The Little Prince

First American edition published in 2012 by Graphic Universe™.

Le Petit Prince ™

based on the masterpiece by Antoine de Saint-Exupéry

© 2012 LPPM
An animated series based on the novel *Le Petit Prince* by Antoine de Saint-Exupéry
Developed for television by Matthieu Delaporte, Alexandre de la Patellière, and Bertrand Gatignol
Directed by Pierre-Alain Chartier

© 2012 ÉDITIONS GLÉNAT
Copyright © 2012 by Lerner Publishing Group, Inc., for the current edition

Graphic Universe™
A division of Lerner Publishing Group, Inc.
241 First Avenue North
Minneapolis, MN 55401 U.S.A.

Website address: www.lernerbooks.com

Library of Congress Cataloging-in-Publication Data

Dorison, Guillaume.
    [Planète de Jade. English]
    The planet of Jade / by Maud Loisillier and Diane Morel ; adapted by Guillaume Dorison ; based on the masterpiece by Antoine de Saint-Exupéry ; illustrated by Élyum Studio ; translation: Anne Collins Smith and Owen Smith. — 1st American ed.
        p.   cm. — (The little prince ; #04)
    ISBN: 978-0-7613-8754-1 (lib. bdg. : alk. paper) 1. Graphic novels. I. Loisillier, Maud. II. Morel, Diane. III. Smith, Anne Collins. IV. Smith, Owen. V. Saint-Exupéry, Antoine de, 1900-1944. Petit prince. VI. Élyum Studio. VII. Petit Prince (Television program) VIII. Title.
PZ7.7.D67Pgj 2012
741.5'944—dc23   2011051719

Manufactured in the United States of America
1 — DP — 7/15/12

THE NEW ADVENTURES
BASED ON THE MASTERPIECE BY ANTOINE DE SAINT-EXUPÉRY

The Little Prince

THE PLANET OF JADE

Based on the animated series and an original story by Maud Loisillier and Diane Morel

Design: Élyum Studio
Adaptation: Guillaume Dorison
Artistic Direction: Didier Poli
Art: Zedarkcrystal
Backgrounds: Isa Python
Coloring: Karine Lambin
Editing: Marco Allard
Editorial Consultant: Didier Convard

Translation: Anne and Owen Smith

Graphic Universe™ • Minneapolis • New York

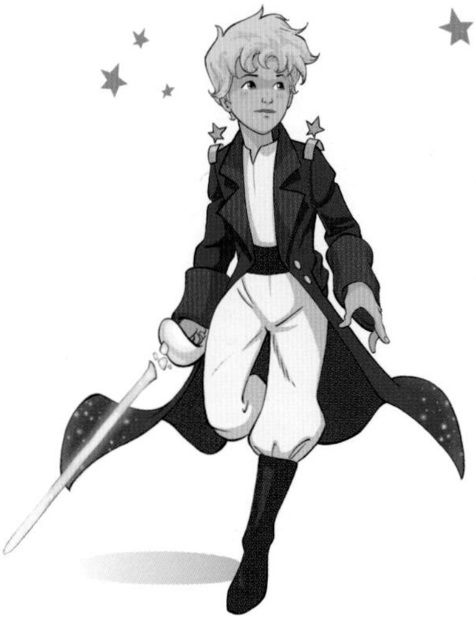

★ THE LITTLE PRINCE

The Little Prince has extraordinary gifts. His sense of wonder allows him to discover what no one else can see. The Little Prince can communicate with all the beings in the universe, even the animals and plants. His powers grow over the course of his adventures.

The Prince's uniform:
When he wears the uniform of a prince, he is more agile and quick. When faced with difficult situations, the Little Prince also carries a sword that lets him sketch and bring to life anything from his imagination.

His sketchbook:
When he is not in his Prince's clothing, the Little Prince carries a sketchbook. When he blows on the pages, they take wing and form objects that he'll find very useful. Like his sword, it's powered by stardust collected on his travels.

★ FOX

A grouch, a trickster, and, so he says, interested only in his next meal, Fox is in reality the Little Prince's best friend. As such, he is always there to give him help, but also just as much to help him to grow and to learn about the world.

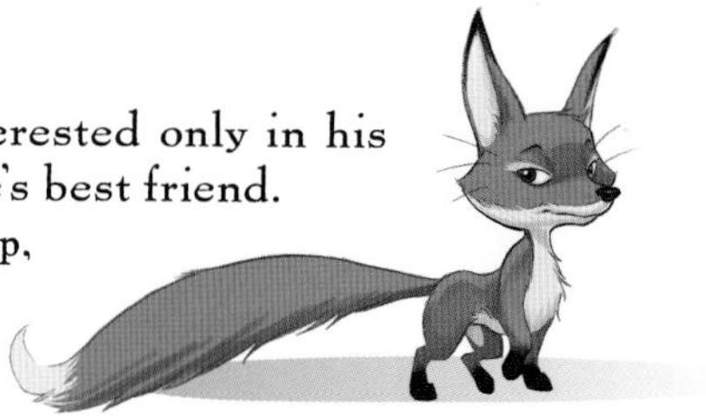

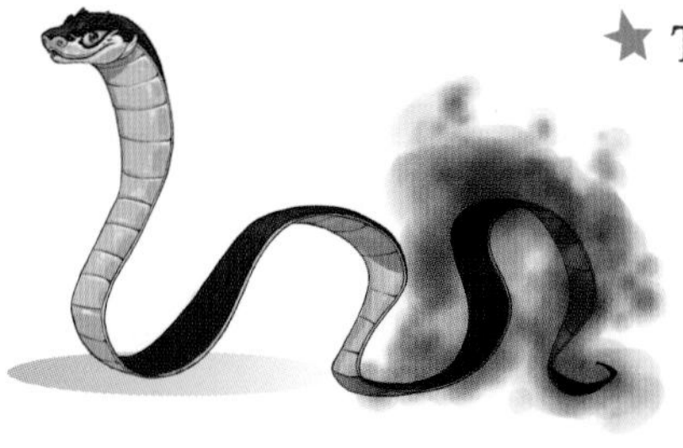

★ THE SNAKE

Even though the Little Prince still does not know exactly why, there can be no doubt that the Snake has set his mind to plunging the entire universe into darkness! And to accomplish his goal, this malicious being is ready to use any form of deception. However, the Snake never takes action himself. He prefers to bring out the wickedness in those beings he has chosen to bite, tempting them to put their own worlds in danger.

★ THE GLOOMIES

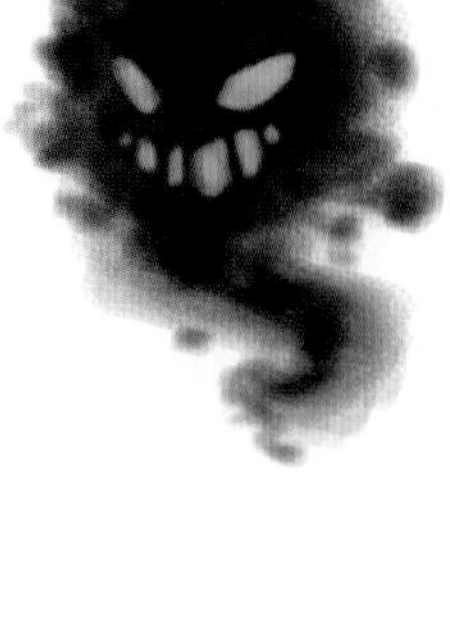

When people who have been "bitten" by the Snake have completely destroyed their own planets, they become Gloomies, slaves to their Snake master. The Gloomies act as a group and carry out the Snake's most vile orders so as to get the better of the Little Prince!

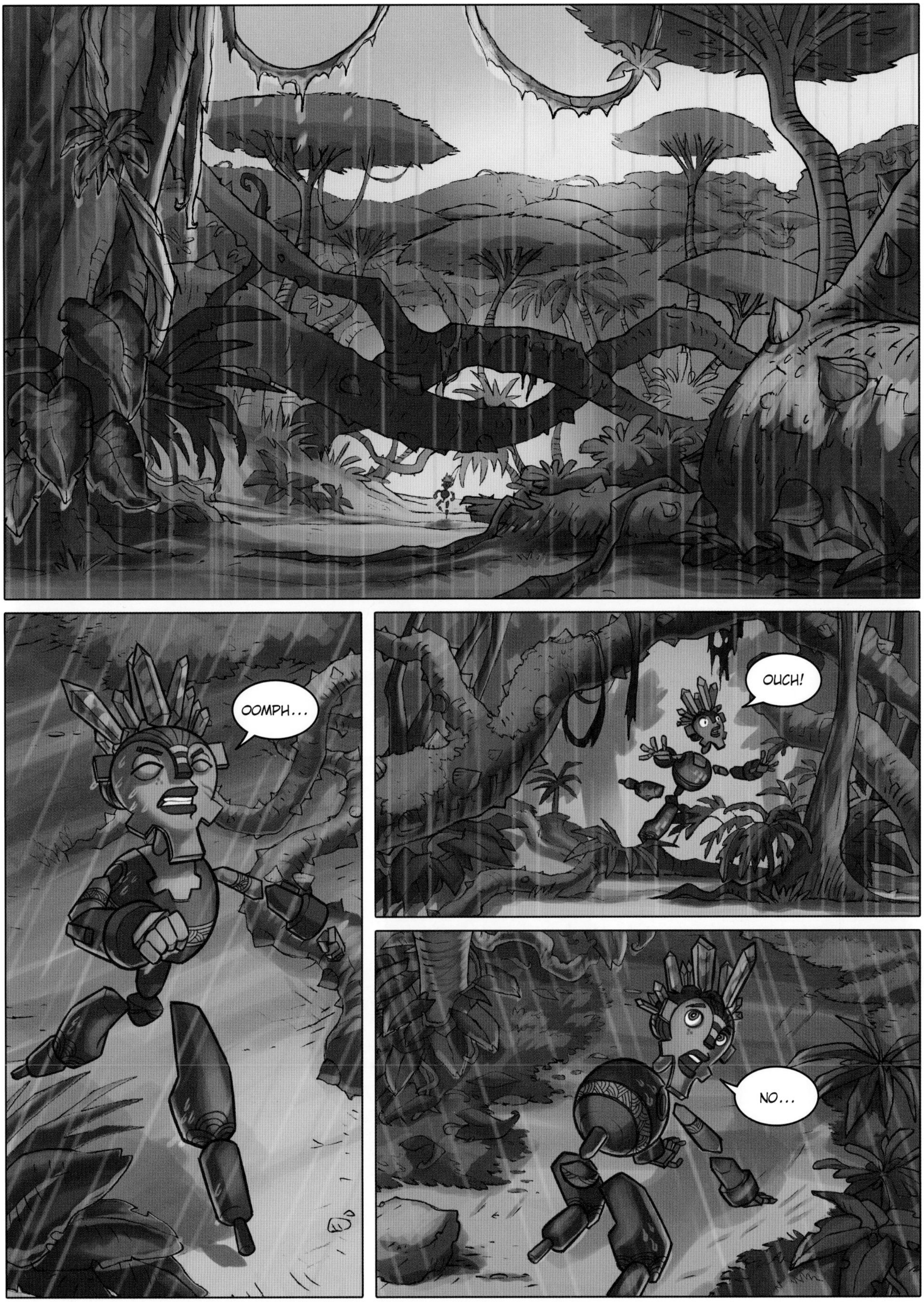
OOMPH...
OUCH!
NO...

AAAAH!

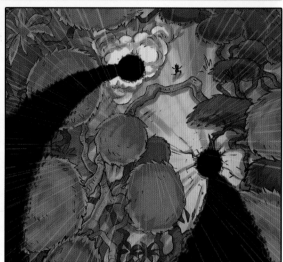

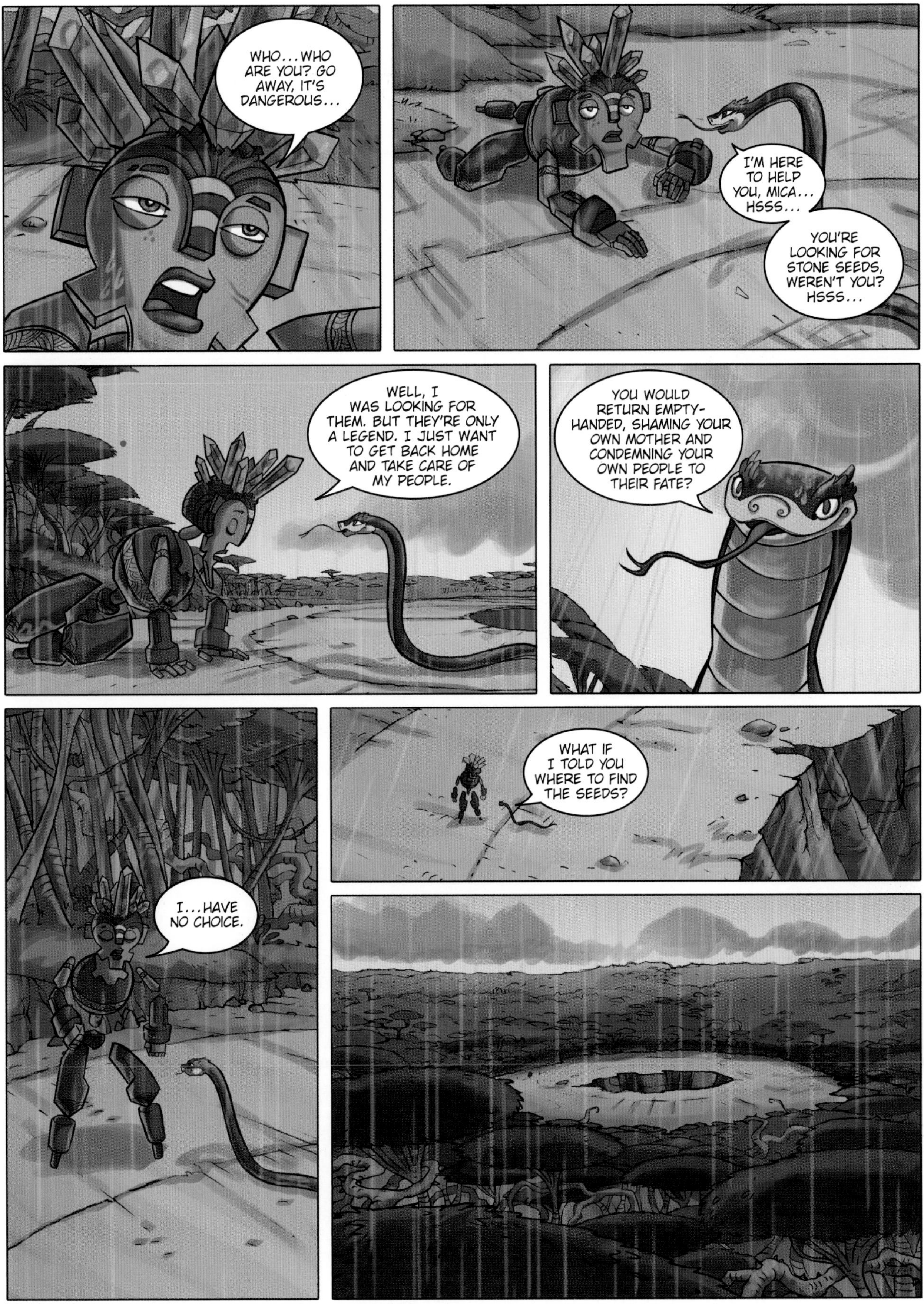
WHO...WHO ARE YOU? GO AWAY, IT'S DANGEROUS...
I'M HERE TO HELP YOU, MICA... HSSS...
YOU'RE LOOKING FOR STONE SEEDS, WEREN'T YOU? HSSS...
WELL, I WAS LOOKING FOR THEM. BUT THEY'RE ONLY A LEGEND. I JUST WANT TO GET BACK HOME AND TAKE CARE OF MY PEOPLE.
YOU WOULD RETURN EMPTY-HANDED, SHAMING YOUR OWN MOTHER AND CONDEMNING YOUR OWN PEOPLE TO THEIR FATE?
WHAT IF I TOLD YOU WHERE TO FIND THE SEEDS?
I...HAVE NO CHOICE.

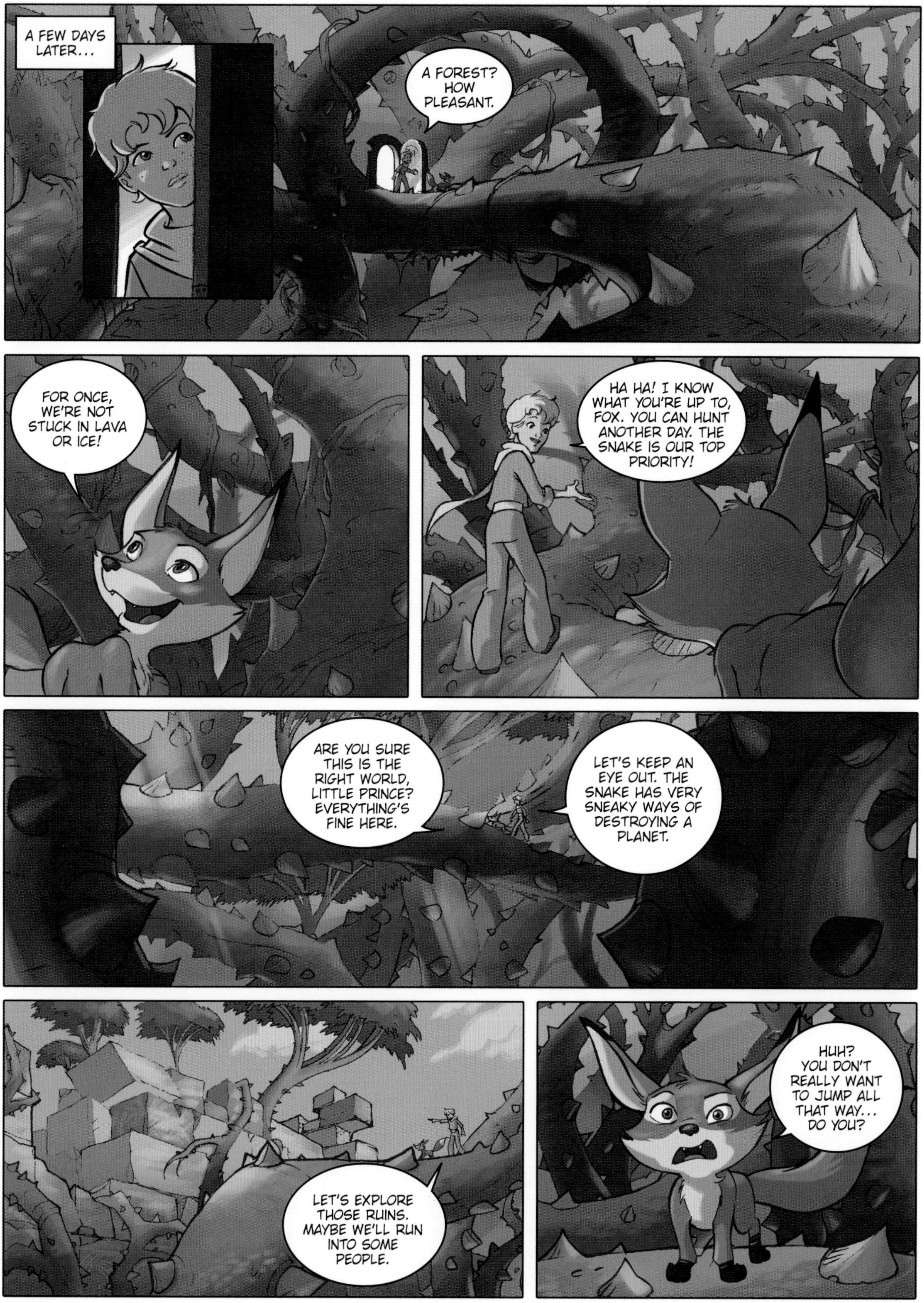
A FEW DAYS LATER...
A FOREST? HOW PLEASANT.
FOR ONCE, WE'RE NOT STUCK IN LAVA OR ICE!
HA HA! I KNOW WHAT YOU'RE UP TO, FOX. YOU CAN HUNT ANOTHER DAY. THE SNAKE IS OUR TOP PRIORITY!
ARE YOU SURE THIS IS THE RIGHT WORLD, LITTLE PRINCE? EVERYTHING'S FINE HERE.
LET'S KEEP AN EYE OUT. THE SNAKE HAS VERY SNEAKY WAYS OF DESTROYING A PLANET.
LET'S EXPLORE THOSE RUINS. MAYBE WE'LL RUN INTO SOME PEOPLE.
HUH? YOU DON'T REALLY WANT TO JUMP ALL THAT WAY... DO YOU?

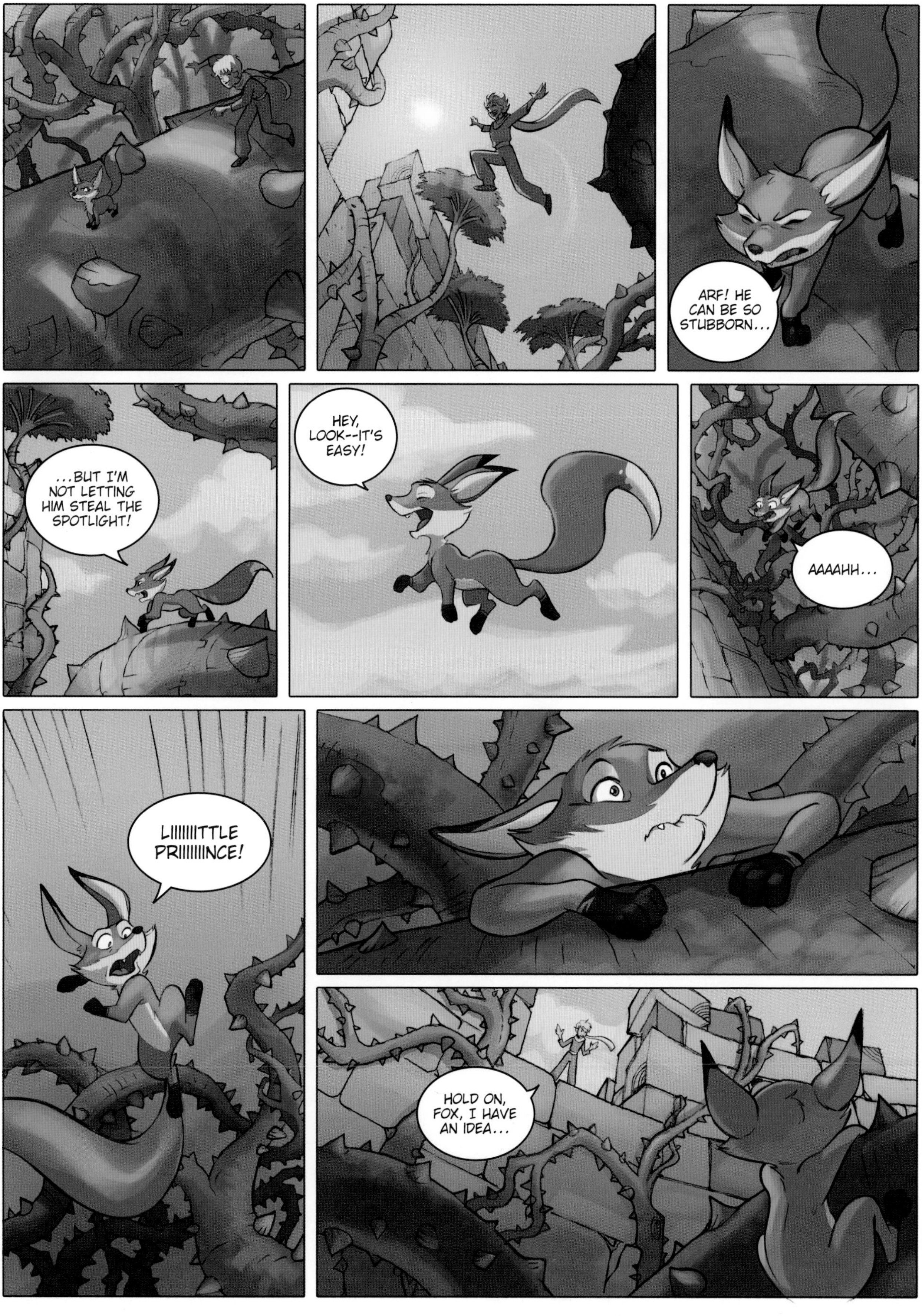
ARF! HE CAN BE SO STUBBORN...
...BUT I'M NOT LETTING HIM STEAL THE SPOTLIGHT!
HEY, LOOK--IT'S EASY!
AAAAHH...
LIIIIIITTLE PRIIIIIINCE!
HOLD ON, FOX, I HAVE AN IDEA...

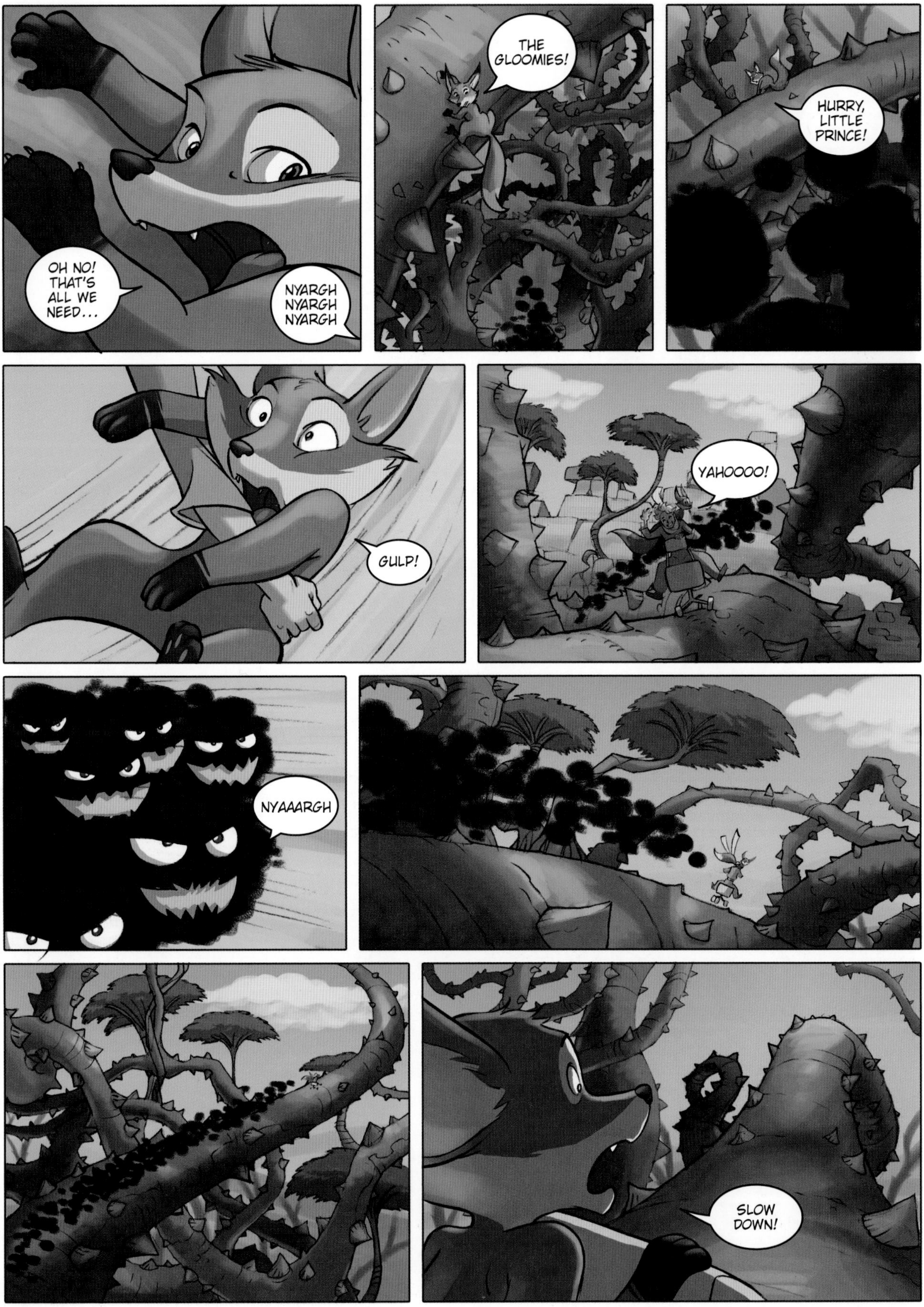
OH NO! THAT'S ALL WE NEED...
NYARGH NYARGH NYARGH
THE GLOOMIES!
HURRY, LITTLE PRINCE!
GULP!
YAHOOOO!
NYAAARGH
SLOW DOWN!

MICA?

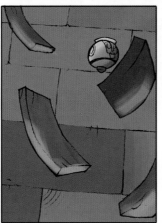

WHAT'S YOUR NEXT BRIGHT IDEA? USE A BOAT TO CUT THROUGH THE BRAMBLES OR MAYBE AN UMBRELLA?

THANKS FOR THE HELP, BUT THE GLOOMIES MIGHT'VE TREATED ME BETTER.

HAH! LOOK!

MICA, MICA? IS IT YOU?

THANKS FOR HELPING US.

I'M SO SORRY. I MISTOOK YOU FOR SOMEONE ELSE.

SEE, I'M STILL RIGHT-- YOU'RE NOT THE ONE HE CAME TO SAVE.

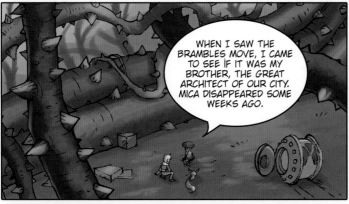

WHEN I SAW THE BRAMBLES MOVE, I CAME TO SEE IF IT WAS MY BROTHER, THE GREAT ARCHITECT OF OUR CITY. MICA DISAPPEARED SOME WEEKS AGO.

MY NAME IS NICKEL, OF THE LITHIAN PEOPLE. PEOPLE OF STONE, PROUD OF OUR OWN!

PLEASED TO MEET YOU. I'M THE LITTLE PRINCE, AND THIS IS MY FRIEND FOX.

LET'S HURRY. IT'S NOT SAFE HERE. THE BRAMBLES COULD ATTACK AT ANY MOMENT. I'LL TAKE YOU TO LAZULIS.

WHAT'S THE PROBLEM WITH THE BRAMBLES? HOW COULD NATURE BE YOUR ENEMY?

NATURE'S DESTRUCTIVE--IT'S NOT MADE OF STONE. HOW COULD YOU NOT KNOW THAT?

HE COMES FROM A TINY PLANET WHERE THE ENTIRE PLANT LIFE IS A SINGLE ROSE. OUR LITTLE PRINCE IS A BIT OUT OF TOUCH.

DON'T BE AFRAID. YOU'LL SOON BE SAFE BEHIND OUR WALLS.

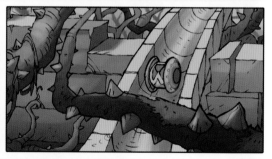

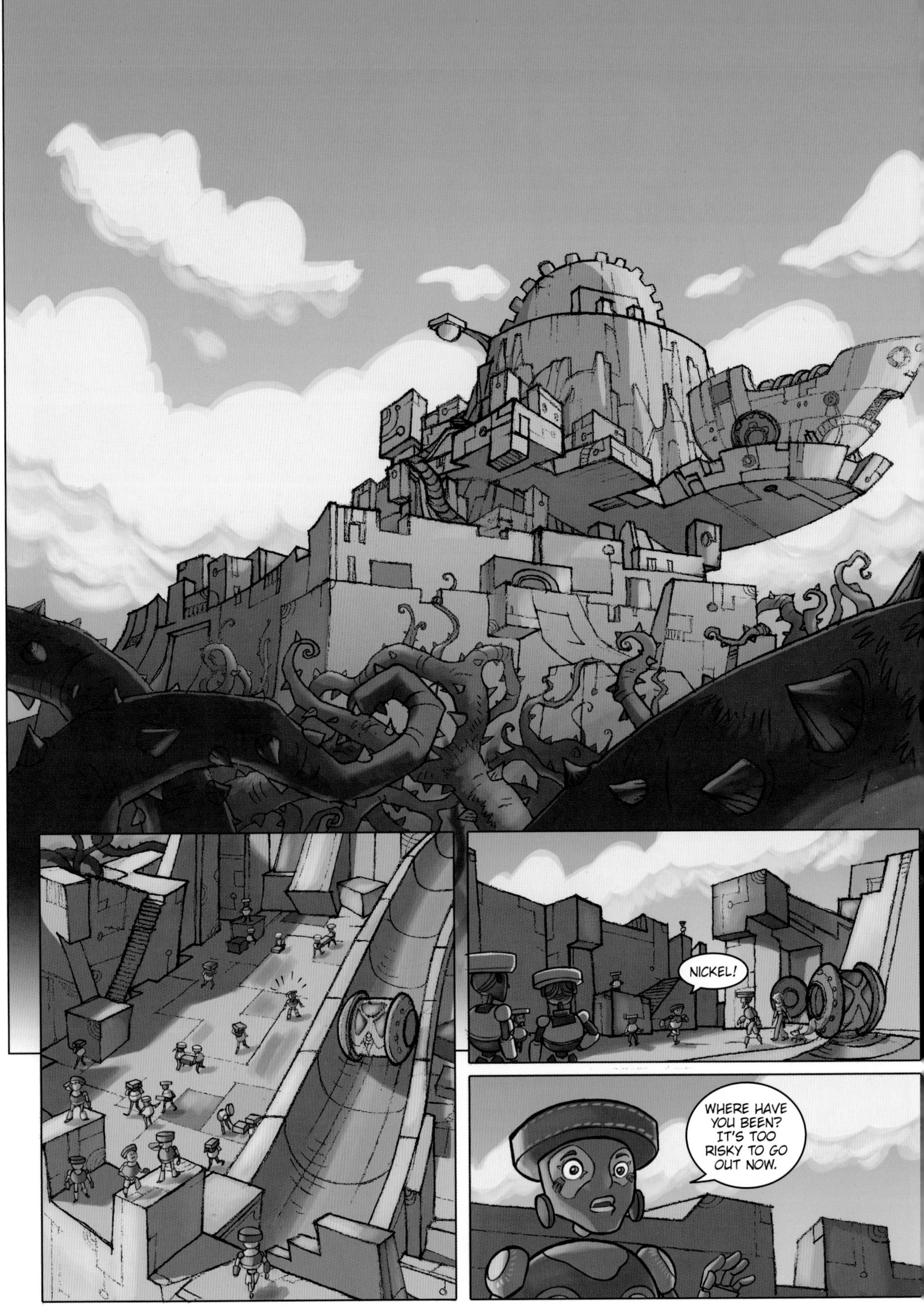
NICKEL!
WHERE HAVE YOU BEEN? IT'S TOO RISKY TO GO OUT NOW.

SWEETHEART, LET ME INTRODUCE THE LITTLE PRINCE AND HIS FRIEND FOX.

I RESCUED THEM FROM THE BRAMBLES.

HELLO, LITTLE PRINCE AND HIS FOUR-FOOTED FRIEND.

THIS IS MY GIRLFRIEND...MY LITTLE DIAMOND... ONYX.

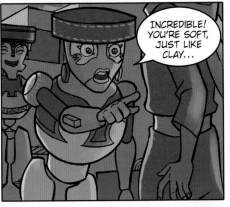

INCREDIBLE! YOU'RE SOFT, JUST LIKE CLAY...

YES, YES... STOP, THAT TICKLES!

GREAT, YOU'RE ALREADY MAKING NEW FRIENDS.

DON'T WE HAVE A SNAKE TO CATCH?

HA HA...YES, I'M SORRY. FOX IS RIGHT.

WHAT'S GOING ON HERE? ARE THE BRAMBLES CONNECTED TO MICA'S DISAPPEARANCE?

MY BROTHER MICA BUILT THIS CITY, LAZULIS, TO PROTECT US FROM THE ENDLESS ATTACKS OF THE BRAMBLES.

BUT HE REALIZED THAT OUR RAMPARTS WOULDN'T HOLD FOREVER.

THE BRAMBLES ARE GETTING MORE AND MORE AGGRESSIVE, SO MY BROTHER LEFT TO LOOK FOR THE MAGICAL STONE SEEDS. ACCORDING TO LEGEND, THEY WOULD ENABLE US TO BUILD GIGANTIC WALLS. BUT WE'VE HAD NO NEWS OF HIM.

I SEE. BUT WHY HAVE THE BRAMBLES SUDDENLY BECOME SO VIOLENT? COULDN'T THE SNAKE BE BEHIND ALL THIS?

WHAT'S HAPPENING?

IS IT DINNERTIME?

IT'S THE ALARM. THE BRAMBLES ARE ATTACKING!

HURRY! WE MUST SEAL THE BREACHES!

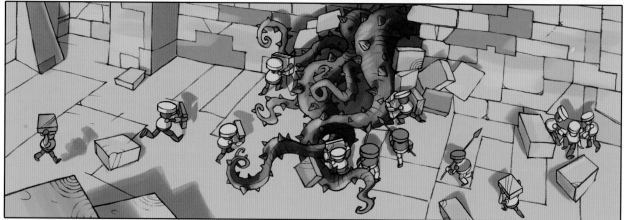

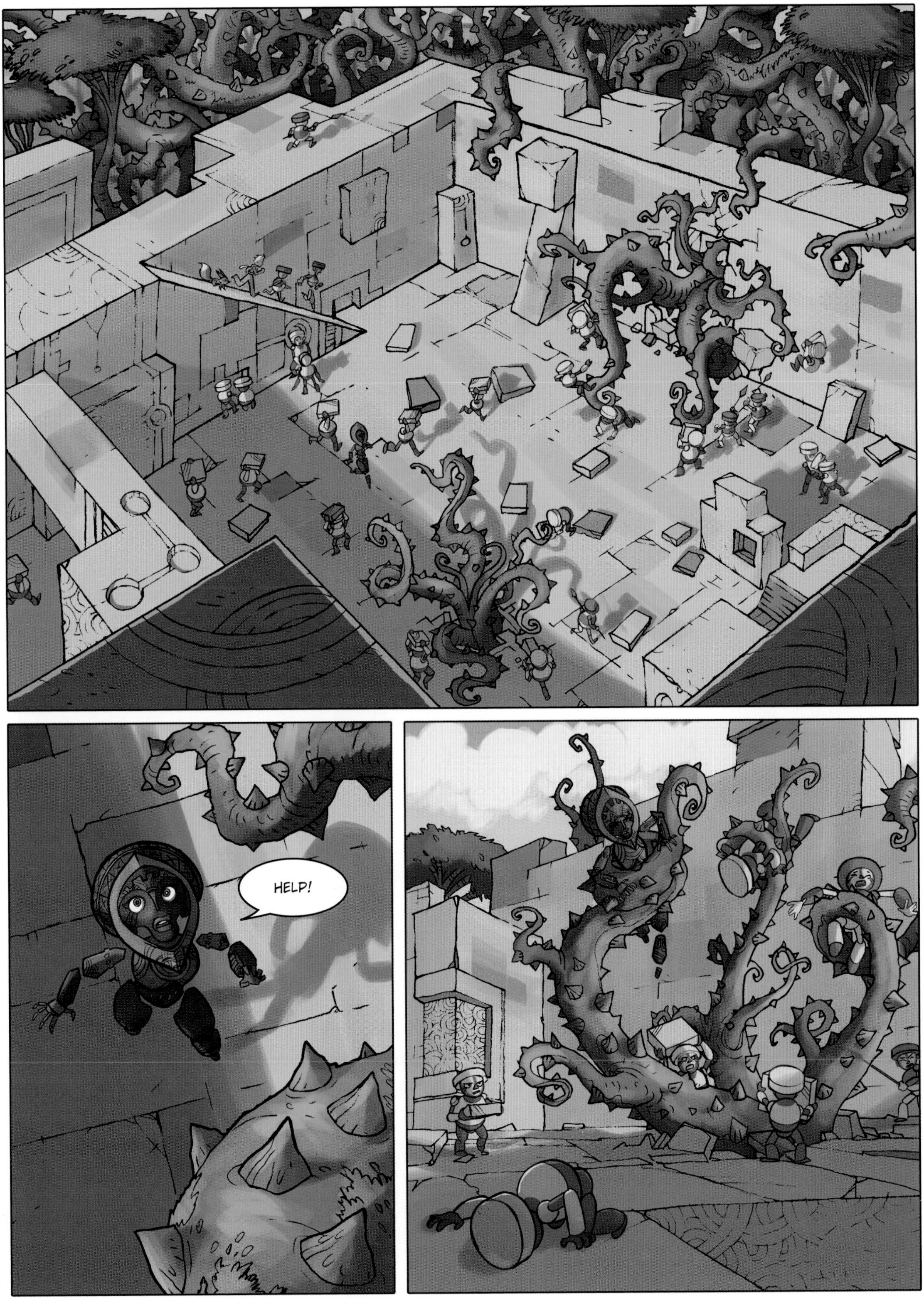
HELP!

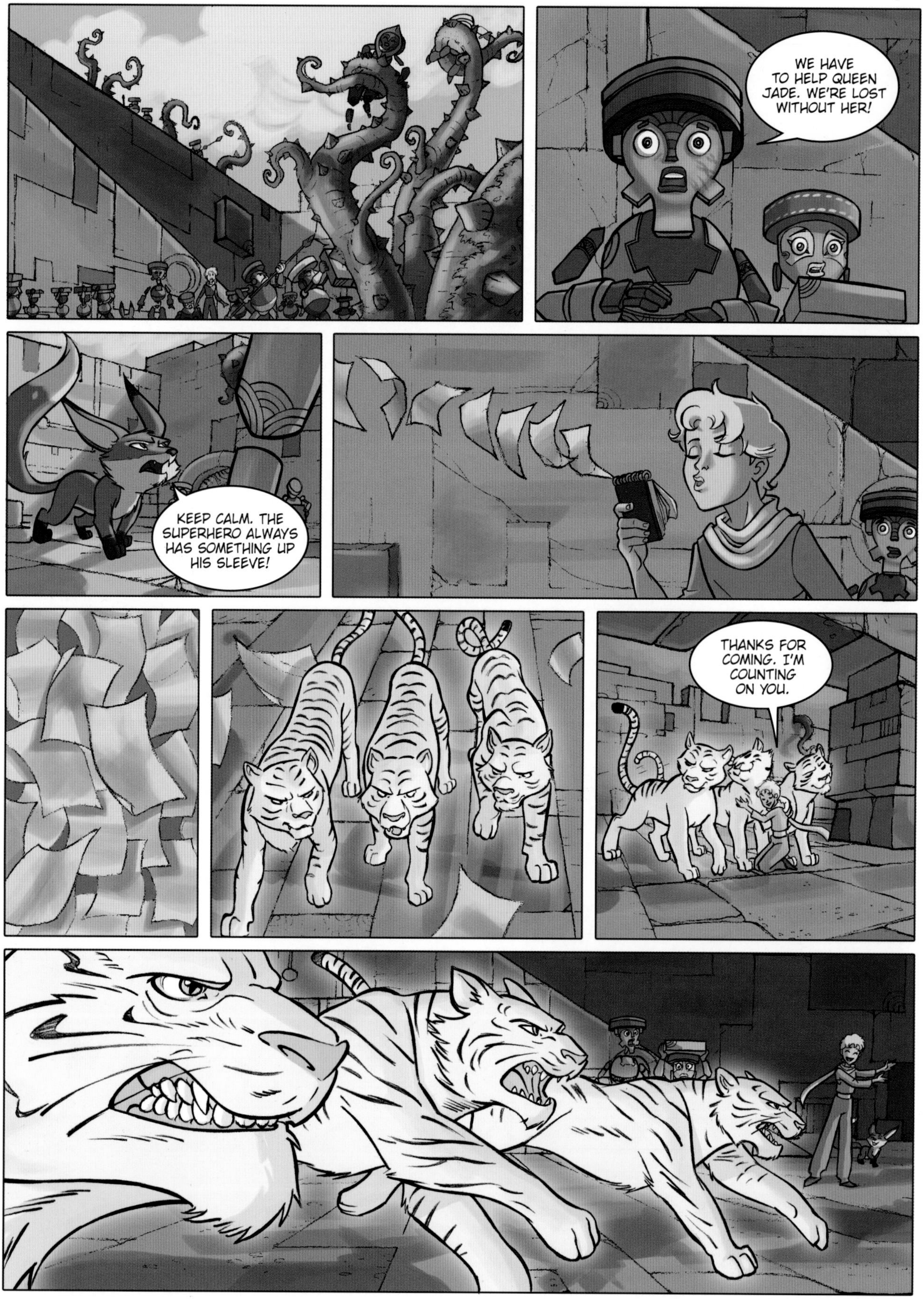
WE HAVE TO HELP QUEEN JADE. WE'RE LOST WITHOUT HER!
KEEP CALM. THE SUPERHERO ALWAYS HAS SOMETHING UP HIS SLEEVE!
THANKS FOR COMING. I'M COUNTING ON YOU.

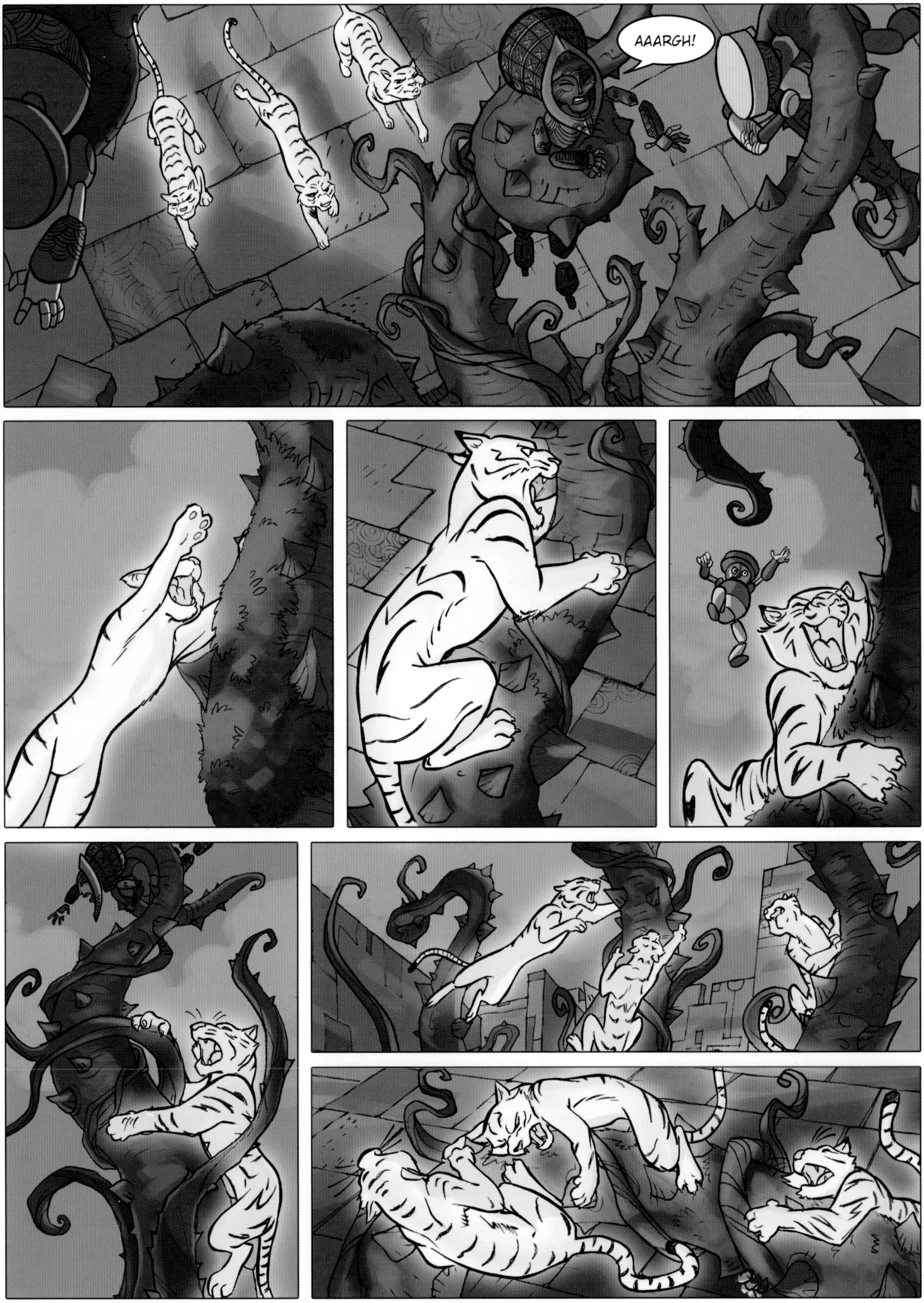
AAARGH!

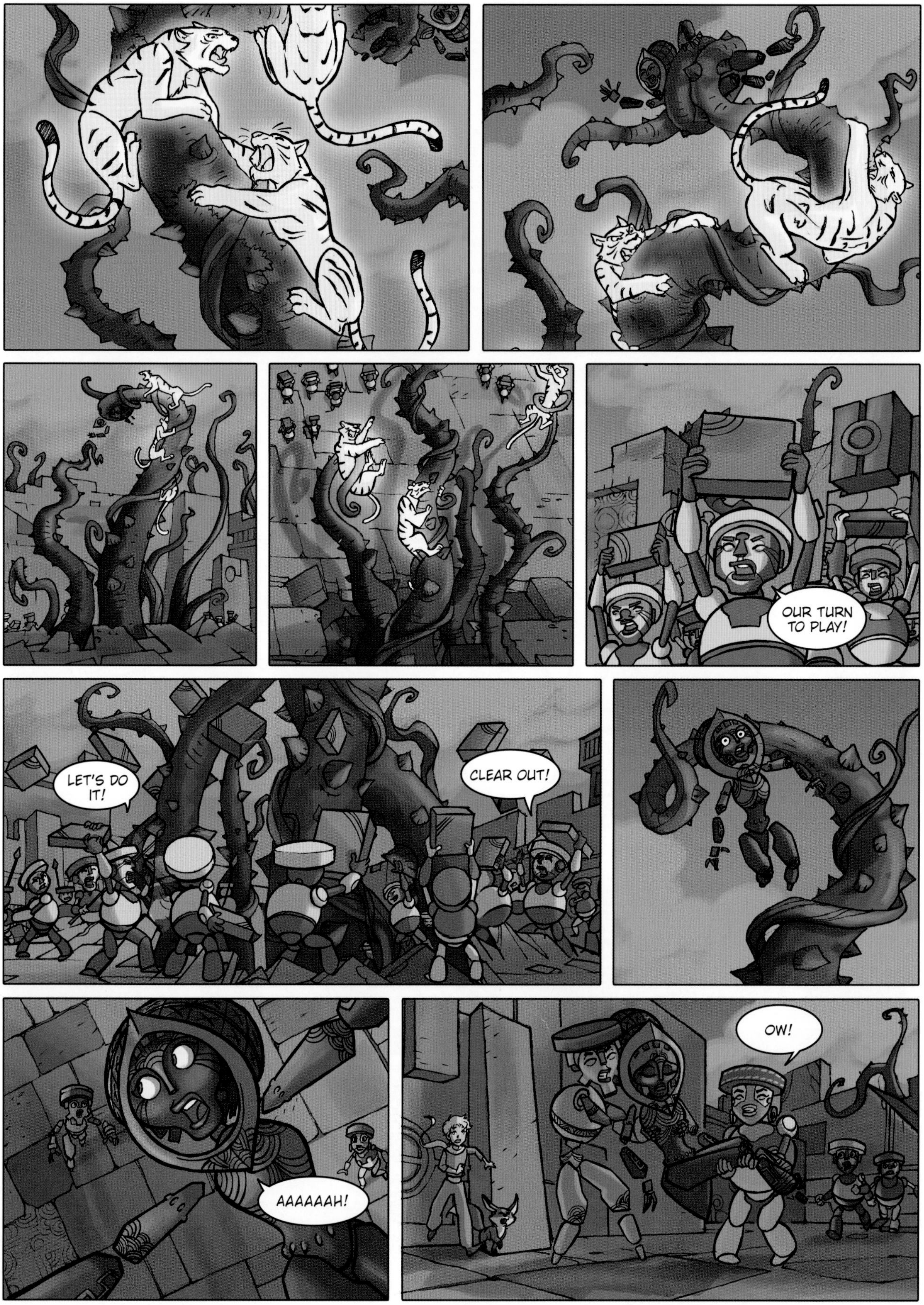
OUR TURN TO PLAY!
LET'S DO IT!
CLEAR OUT!
AAAAAAH!
OW!

MOTHER, ARE YOU ALL RIGHT?

I DON'T KNOW WHERE YOU CAME FROM, BUT THANK YOU FOR FIGHTING ON OUR SIDE.

THANK YOU, JADE, FOR YOUR HOSPITALITY.

DO THESE ATTACKS HAPPEN OFTEN? WHY DON'T YOU FIND A SAFER PLACE TO LIVE?

WHY SHOULD WE ABANDON OUR OWN LANDS? WE HAVE A RIGHT TO LIVE HERE AND WE WON'T LET THOSE WICKED BRAMBLES OVERRUN US.

MICA WILL SOON RETURN WITH THE STONE SEEDS. UNTIL THEN, YOUR WHITE TIGERS CAN PROTECT US.

SHE HAS A POINT, DOESN'T SHE, LITTLE PRINCE?

PARDON ME, JADE, BUT IF YOU DON'T KNOW WHERE MICA IS, HOW CAN YOU KNOW WHEN HE'LL RETURN OR EVEN IF HE'LL FIND THOSE SEEDS? ISN'T IT MORE IMPORTANT TO GET YOUR PEOPLE TO SAFETY?

I KNOW MY SON WILL BE HERE SOON, AND NO ONE'S LEAVING UNTIL HE GETS BACK!

THEN WHY NOT GO LOOK FOR HIM?

I STILL HAVE MY FLYING ARCH. WE COULD USE IT TO FIND MICA.

A BROKEN MACHINE IS USELESS.

YOU SHOULD BE MORE LIKE YOUR BROTHER. HE BUILT MAGNIFICENT CITIES.

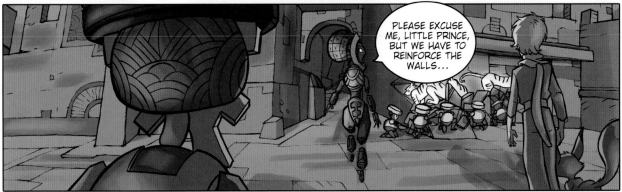

PLEASE EXCUSE ME, LITTLE PRINCE, BUT WE HAVE TO REINFORCE THE WALLS...

WHAT SHOULD I DO? WAIT FOR MY BELOVED SON, AS I PROMISED? OR LEAVE, AS MY PEOPLE WISH?

WHY DON'T YOU ANSWER ME? I DID WHAT YOU TOLD ME TO DO, BUT THINGS HAVE GOTTEN WORSE!

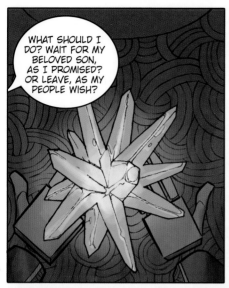

I NEVER TOLD YOU TO DO ANYTHING, QUEEN JADE... HSSS...I JUST CLARIFIED THE SITUATION, AND YOU DREW YOUR OWN CONCLUSIONS.

WELL, THEN, INSPIRE ME ONCE AGAIN, SNAKE.

HSSS...TO LEAVE OR NOT TO LEAVE? THAT IS THE QUESTION. LOOK INSIDE YOUR HEART! HAVE FAITH IN THE SON YOU'VE ALWAYS FAVORED. HOW CAN YOU BETRAY YOUR OWN SON?

IF I RETURN THIS CRYSTAL TO NICKEL, HE COULD USE THE ARCH TO FIND HIS BROTHER!

HSSS...EVEN IF THE MACHINE WORKS, HOW DO YOU PLAN TO FIND MICA IN THAT TRACKLESS FOREST?

THE LITHIANS WILL WANT TO FLEE NOW THAT NICKEL AND HIS NEW FRIENDS TALK OF NOTHING ELSE...

WHY NOT PLAY ON THEIR HOPES?

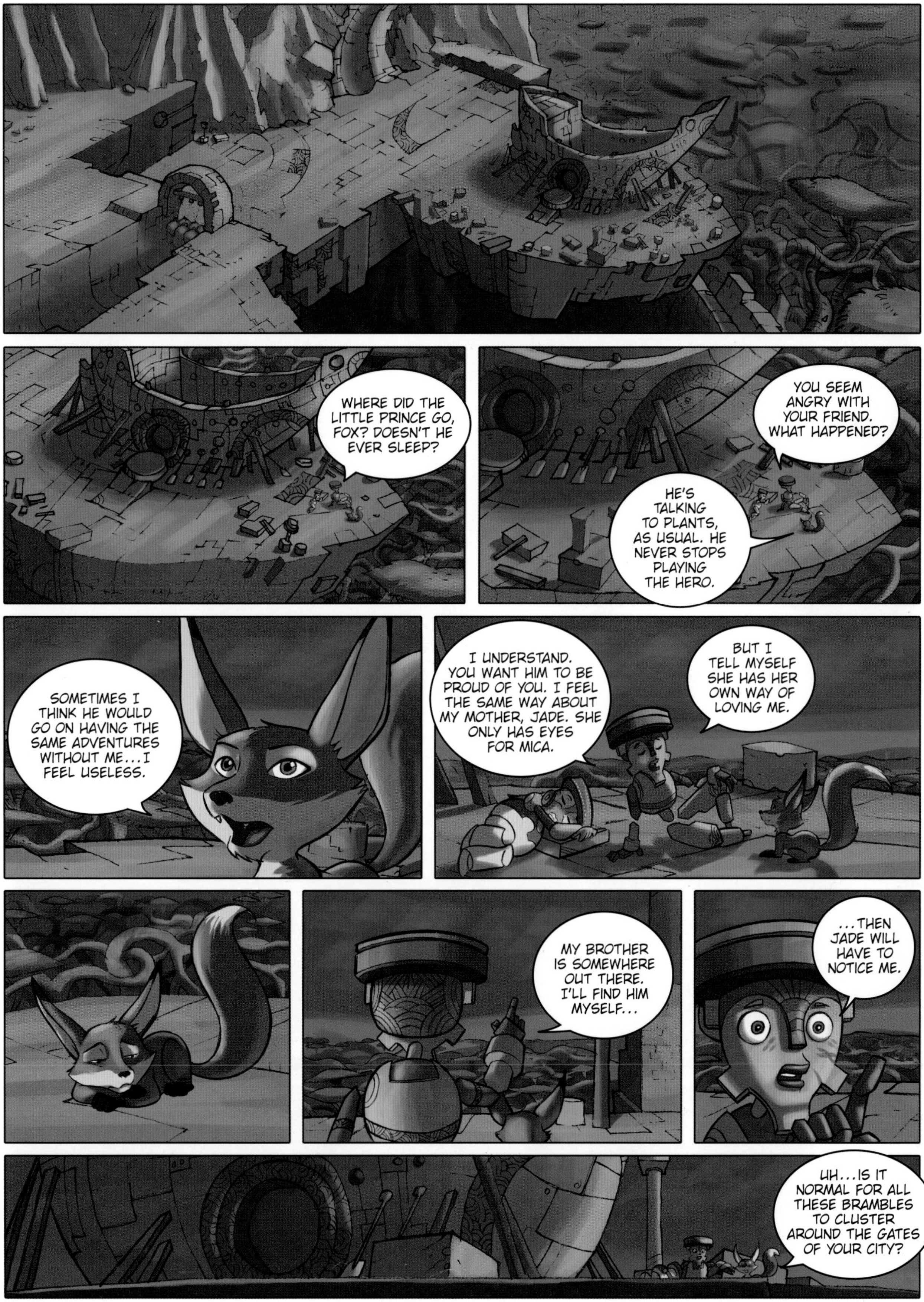
WHERE DID THE LITTLE PRINCE GO, FOX? DOESN'T HE EVER SLEEP?
YOU SEEM ANGRY WITH YOUR FRIEND. WHAT HAPPENED?
HE'S TALKING TO PLANTS, AS USUAL. HE NEVER STOPS PLAYING THE HERO.
SOMETIMES I THINK HE WOULD GO ON HAVING THE SAME ADVENTURES WITHOUT ME... I FEEL USELESS.
I UNDERSTAND. YOU WANT HIM TO BE PROUD OF YOU. I FEEL THE SAME WAY ABOUT MY MOTHER, JADE. SHE ONLY HAS EYES FOR MICA.
BUT I TELL MYSELF SHE HAS HER OWN WAY OF LOVING ME.
MY BROTHER IS SOMEWHERE OUT THERE. I'LL FIND HIM MYSELF...
...THEN JADE WILL HAVE TO NOTICE ME.
UH... IS IT NORMAL FOR ALL THESE BRAMBLES TO CLUSTER AROUND THE GATES OF YOUR CITY?

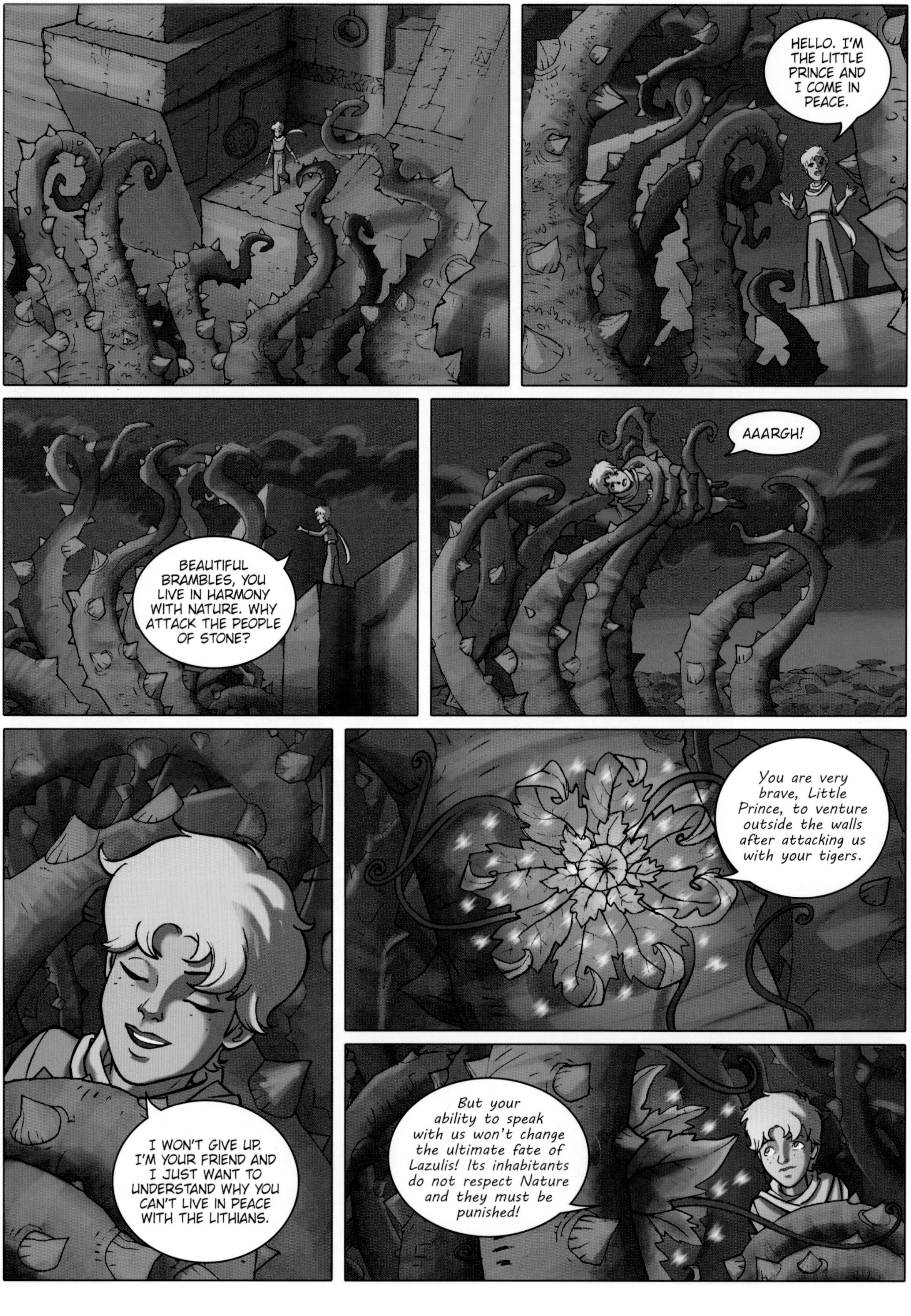
HELLO. I'M THE LITTLE PRINCE AND I COME IN PEACE.
BEAUTIFUL BRAMBLES, YOU LIVE IN HARMONY WITH NATURE. WHY ATTACK THE PEOPLE OF STONE?
AAARGH!
I WON'T GIVE UP. I'M YOUR FRIEND AND I JUST WANT TO UNDERSTAND WHY YOU CAN'T LIVE IN PEACE WITH THE LITHIANS.
You are very brave, Little Prince, to venture outside the walls after attacking us with your tigers.
But your ability to speak with us won't change the ultimate fate of Lazulis! Its inhabitants do not respect Nature and they must be punished!

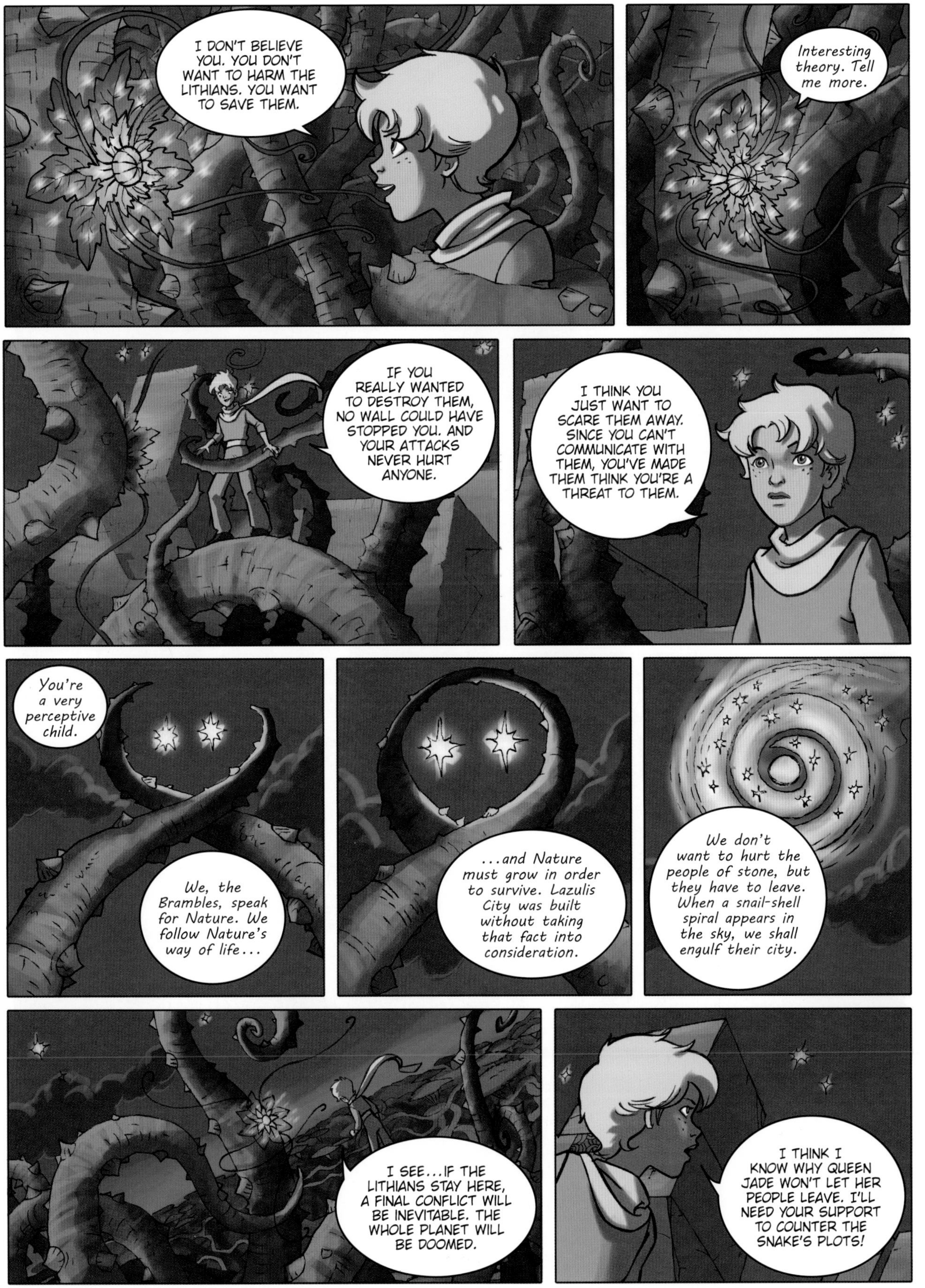
I DON'T BELIEVE YOU. YOU DON'T WANT TO HARM THE LITHIANS. YOU WANT TO SAVE THEM.
Interesting theory. Tell me more.
IF YOU REALLY WANTED TO DESTROY THEM, NO WALL COULD HAVE STOPPED YOU. AND YOUR ATTACKS NEVER HURT ANYONE.
I THINK YOU JUST WANT TO SCARE THEM AWAY. SINCE YOU CAN'T COMMUNICATE WITH THEM, YOU'VE MADE THEM THINK YOU'RE A THREAT TO THEM.
You're a very perceptive child.
We, the Brambles, speak for Nature. We follow Nature's way of life...
...and Nature must grow in order to survive. Lazulis City was built without taking that fact into consideration.
We don't want to hurt the people of stone, but they have to leave. When a snail-shell spiral appears in the sky, we shall engulf their city.
I SEE...IF THE LITHIANS STAY HERE, A FINAL CONFLICT WILL BE INEVITABLE. THE WHOLE PLANET WILL BE DOOMED.
I THINK I KNOW WHY QUEEN JADE WON'T LET HER PEOPLE LEAVE. I'LL NEED YOUR SUPPORT TO COUNTER THE SNAKE'S PLOTS!

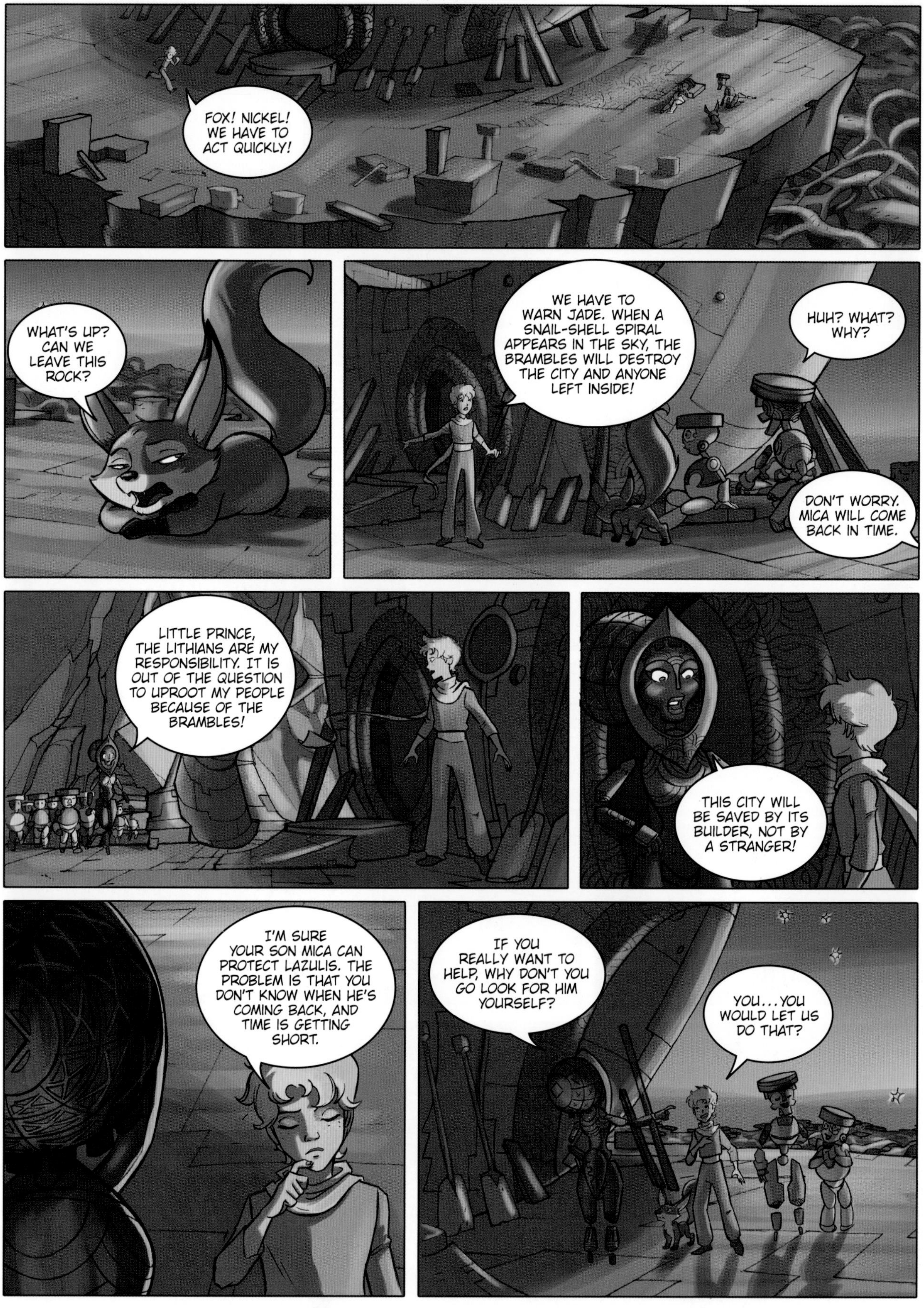
FOX! NICKEL! WE HAVE TO ACT QUICKLY!
WHAT'S UP? CAN WE LEAVE THIS ROCK?
WE HAVE TO WARN JADE. WHEN A SNAIL-SHELL SPIRAL APPEARS IN THE SKY, THE BRAMBLES WILL DESTROY THE CITY AND ANYONE LEFT INSIDE!
HUH? WHAT? WHY?
DON'T WORRY. MICA WILL COME BACK IN TIME.
LITTLE PRINCE, THE LITHIANS ARE MY RESPONSIBILITY. IT IS OUT OF THE QUESTION TO UPROOT MY PEOPLE BECAUSE OF THE BRAMBLES!
THIS CITY WILL BE SAVED BY ITS BUILDER, NOT BY A STRANGER!
I'M SURE YOUR SON MICA CAN PROTECT LAZULIS. THE PROBLEM IS THAT YOU DON'T KNOW WHEN HE'S COMING BACK, AND TIME IS GETTING SHORT.
IF YOU REALLY WANT TO HELP, WHY DON'T YOU GO LOOK FOR HIM YOURSELF?
YOU...YOU WOULD LET US DO THAT?

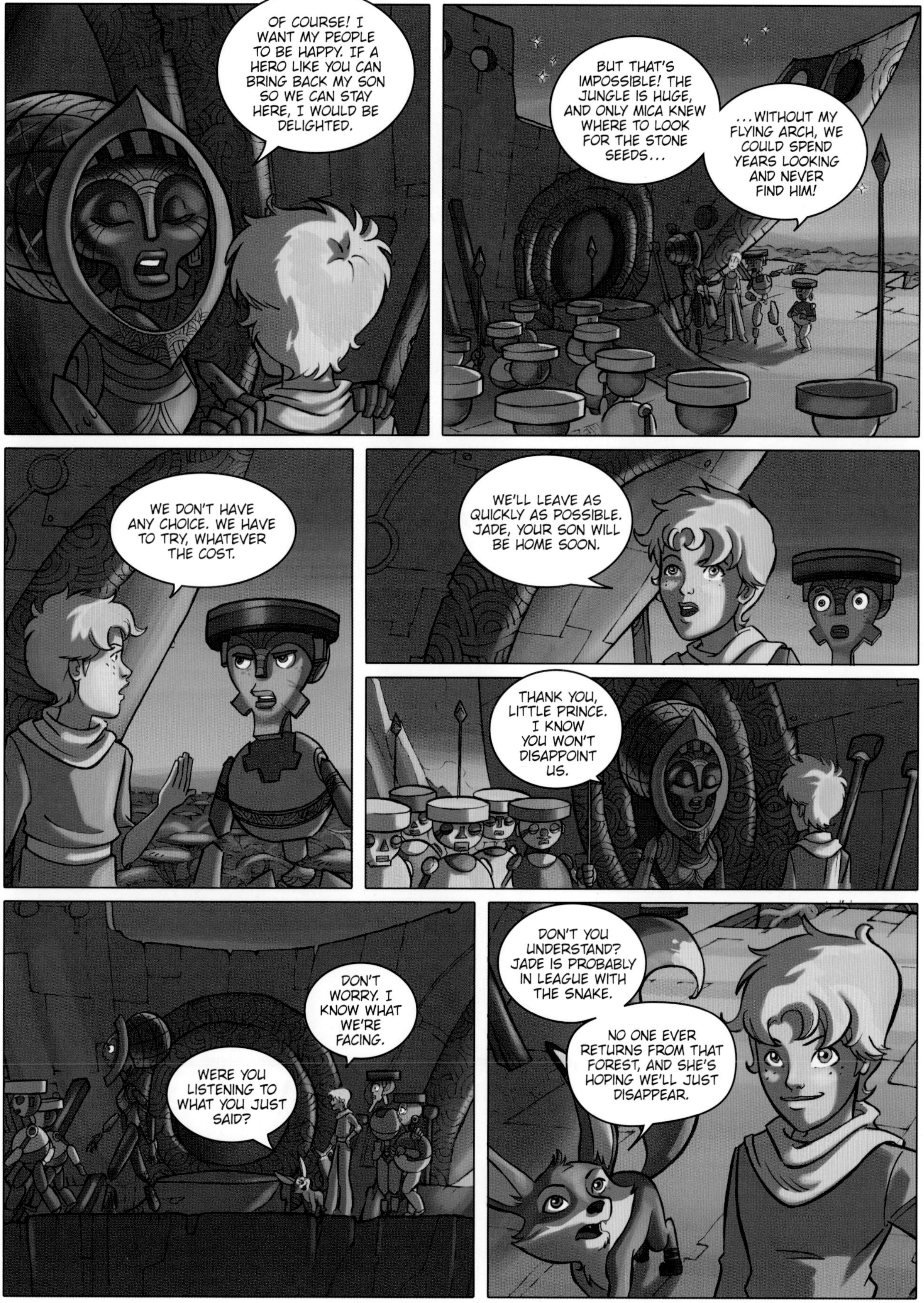
OF COURSE! I WANT MY PEOPLE TO BE HAPPY. IF A HERO LIKE YOU CAN BRING BACK MY SON SO WE CAN STAY HERE, I WOULD BE DELIGHTED.
BUT THAT'S IMPOSSIBLE! THE JUNGLE IS HUGE, AND ONLY MICA KNEW WHERE TO LOOK FOR THE STONE SEEDS...
...WITHOUT MY FLYING ARCH, WE COULD SPEND YEARS LOOKING AND NEVER FIND HIM!
WE DON'T HAVE ANY CHOICE. WE HAVE TO TRY, WHATEVER THE COST.
WE'LL LEAVE AS QUICKLY AS POSSIBLE. JADE, YOUR SON WILL BE HOME SOON.
THANK YOU, LITTLE PRINCE. I KNOW YOU WON'T DISAPPOINT US.
WERE YOU LISTENING TO WHAT YOU JUST SAID?
DON'T WORRY. I KNOW WHAT WE'RE FACING.
DON'T YOU UNDERSTAND? JADE IS PROBABLY IN LEAGUE WITH THE SNAKE.
NO ONE EVER RETURNS FROM THAT FOREST, AND SHE'S HOPING WE'LL JUST DISAPPEAR.

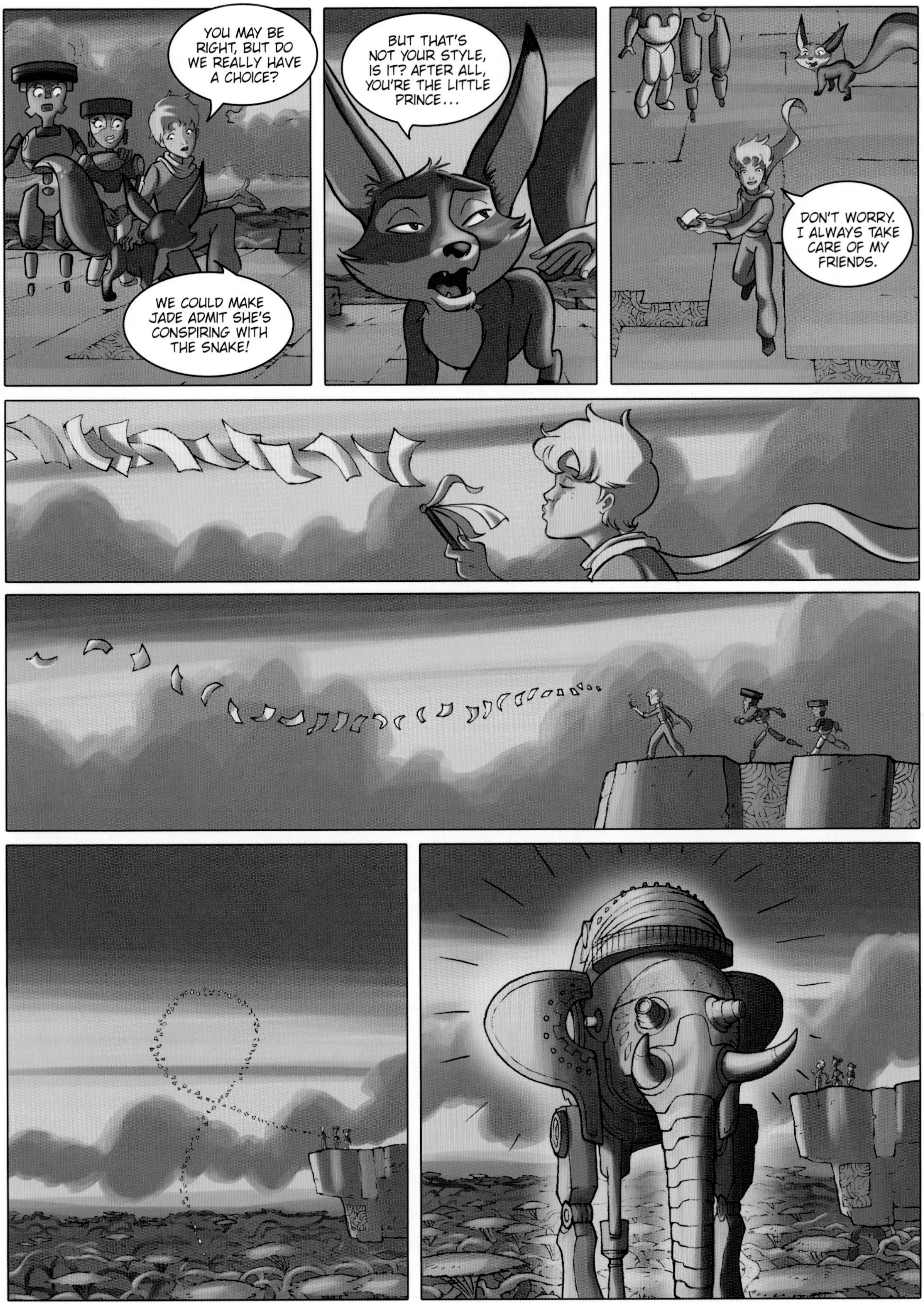
YOU MAY BE RIGHT, BUT DO WE REALLY HAVE A CHOICE?
WE COULD MAKE JADE ADMIT SHE'S CONSPIRING WITH THE SNAKE!
BUT THAT'S NOT YOUR STYLE, IS IT? AFTER ALL, YOU'RE THE LITTLE PRINCE...
DON'T WORRY. I ALWAYS TAKE CARE OF MY FRIENDS.

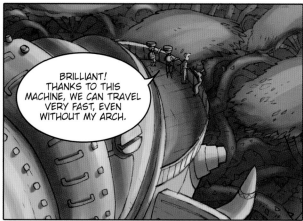

BRILLIANT! THANKS TO THIS MACHINE, WE CAN TRAVEL VERY FAST, EVEN WITHOUT MY ARCH.

BUT THAT STILL LEAVES OUR REAL CHALLENGE...HOW DO WE FIND MICA IN THIS IMMENSE FOREST?

I'VE ASKED THE BRAMBLES TO GET HELP FROM THE TREES IN FINDING MICA.

THAT'S YOUR BIG PLAN? LOOKS LIKE WE'RE NOT GETTING DINNER ANYTIME SOON.

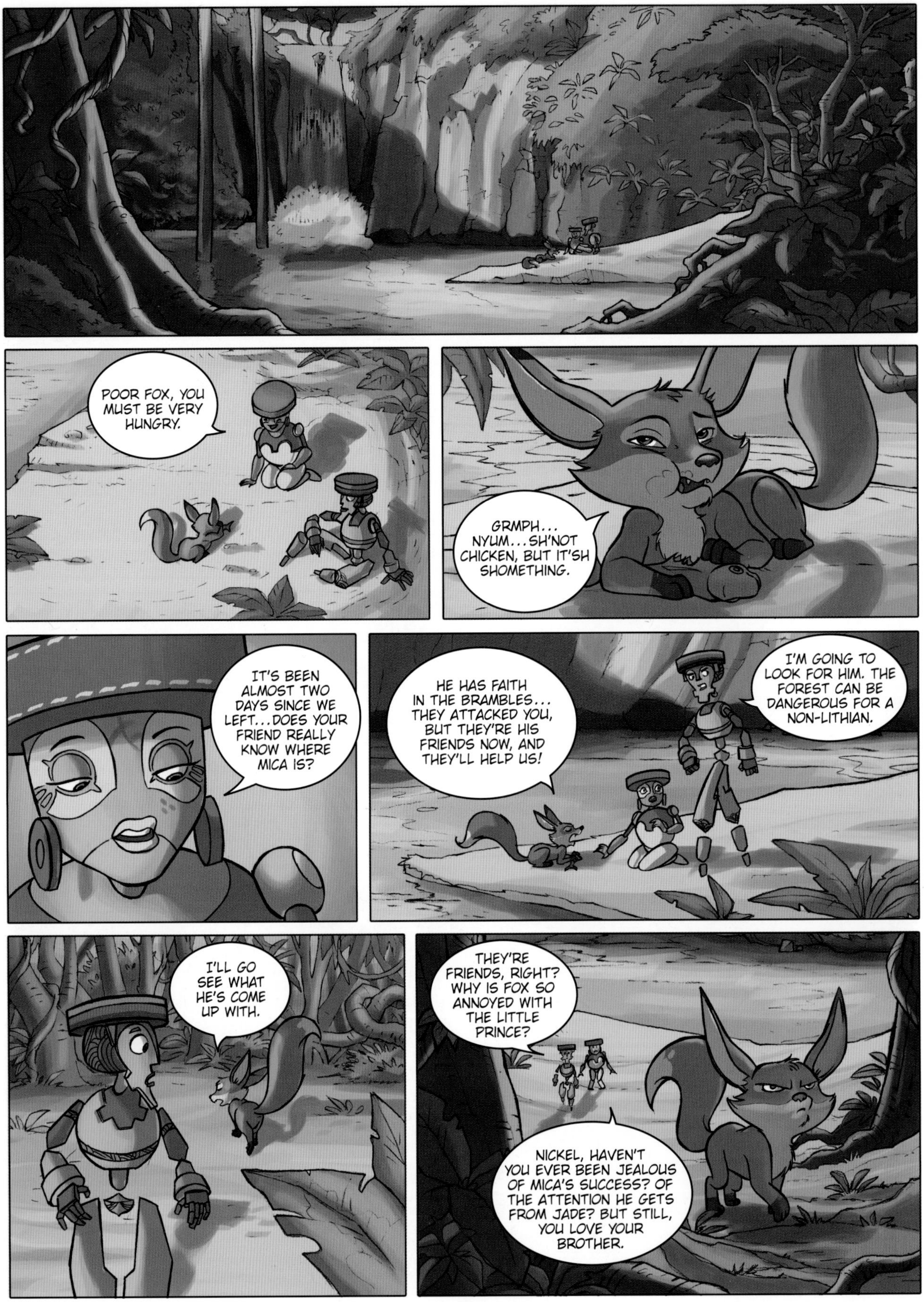
POOR FOX, YOU MUST BE VERY HUNGRY.
GRMPH... NYUM... SH'NOT CHICKEN, BUT IT'SH SHOMETHING.
IT'S BEEN ALMOST TWO DAYS SINCE WE LEFT... DOES YOUR FRIEND REALLY KNOW WHERE MICA IS?
HE HAS FAITH IN THE BRAMBLES... THEY ATTACKED YOU, BUT THEY'RE HIS FRIENDS NOW, AND THEY'LL HELP US!
I'M GOING TO LOOK FOR HIM. THE FOREST CAN BE DANGEROUS FOR A NON-LITHIAN.
I'LL GO SEE WHAT HE'S COME UP WITH.
THEY'RE FRIENDS, RIGHT? WHY IS FOX SO ANNOYED WITH THE LITTLE PRINCE?
NICKEL, HAVEN'T YOU EVER BEEN JEALOUS OF MICA'S SUCCESS? OF THE ATTENTION HE GETS FROM JADE? BUT STILL, YOU LOVE YOUR BROTHER.

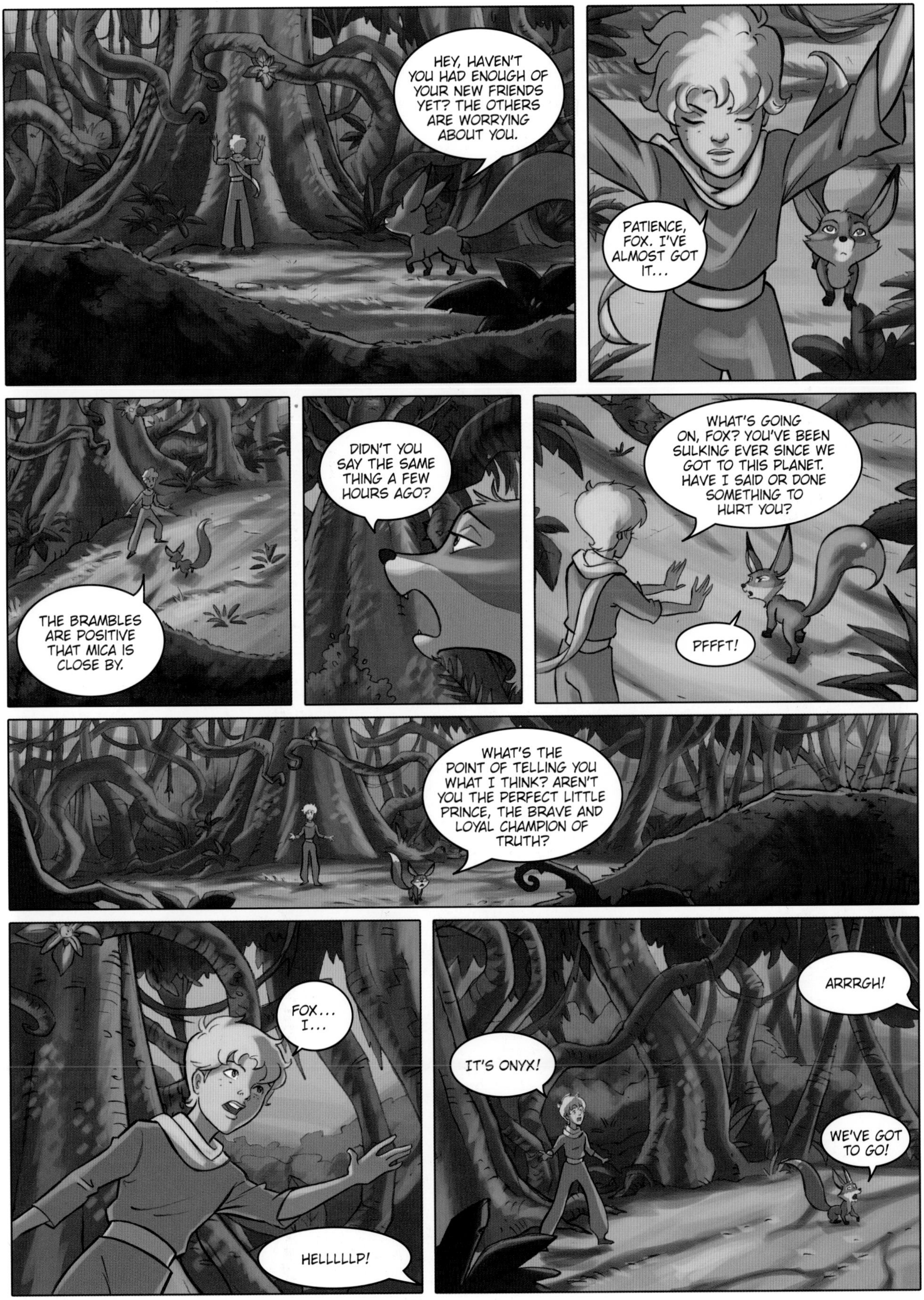
HEY, HAVEN'T YOU HAD ENOUGH OF YOUR NEW FRIENDS YET? THE OTHERS ARE WORRYING ABOUT YOU.
PATIENCE, FOX. I'VE ALMOST GOT IT...
THE BRAMBLES ARE POSITIVE THAT MICA IS CLOSE BY.
DIDN'T YOU SAY THE SAME THING A FEW HOURS AGO?
WHAT'S GOING ON, FOX? YOU'VE BEEN SULKING EVER SINCE WE GOT TO THIS PLANET. HAVE I SAID OR DONE SOMETHING TO HURT YOU?
PFFFT!
WHAT'S THE POINT OF TELLING YOU WHAT I THINK? AREN'T YOU THE PERFECT LITTLE PRINCE, THE BRAVE AND LOYAL CHAMPION OF TRUTH?
FOX... I...
HELLLLLP!
ARRRGH!
IT'S ONYX!
WE'VE GOT TO GO!

WHERE DID
THEY GO?

LOOK OUT!

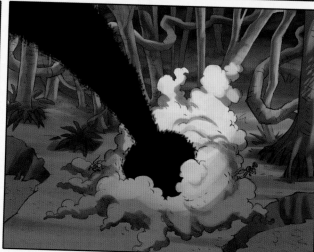

UP
THERE!

WHAT...?

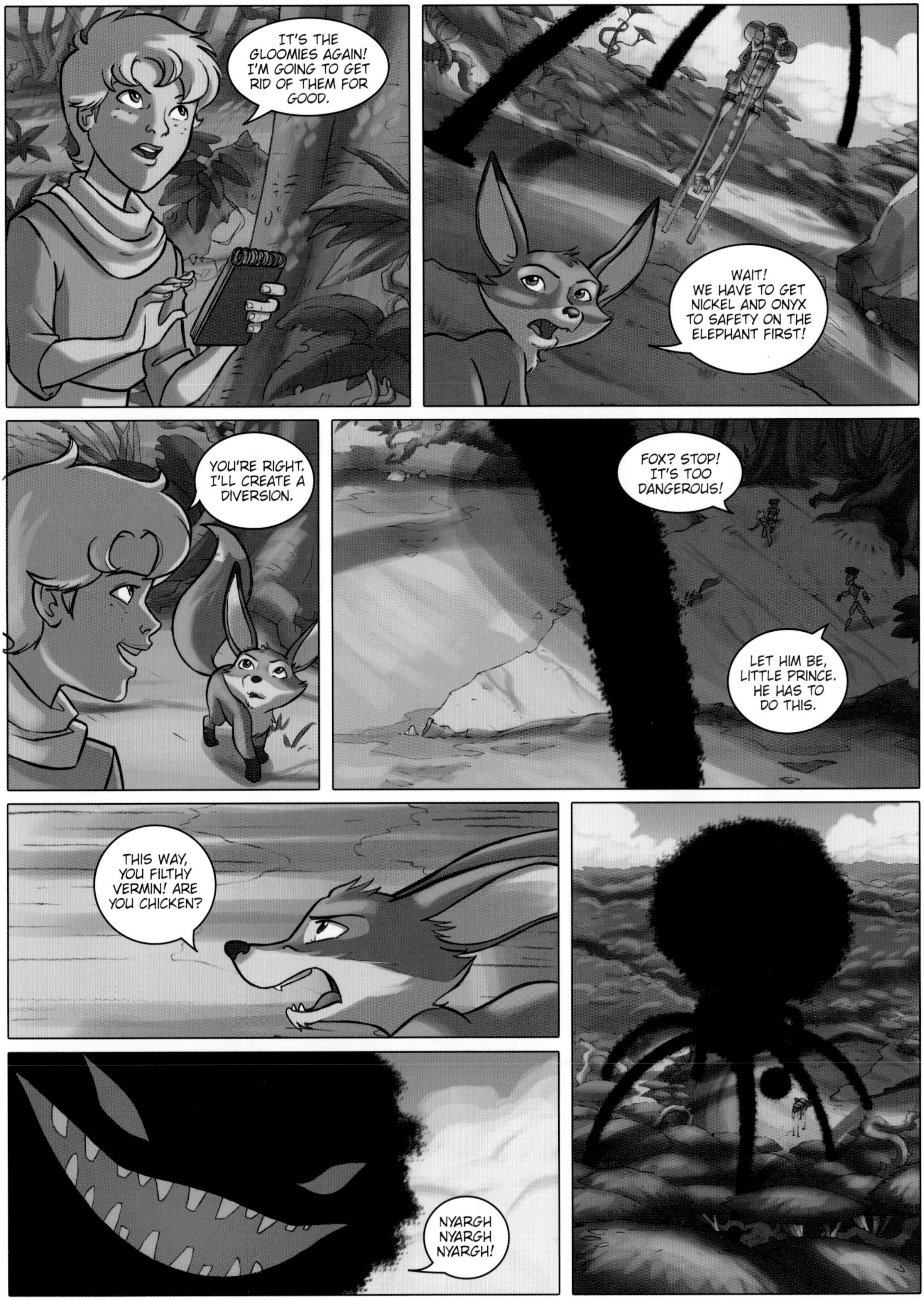
IT'S THE GLOOMIES AGAIN! I'M GOING TO GET RID OF THEM FOR GOOD.
WAIT! WE HAVE TO GET NICKEL AND ONYX TO SAFETY ON THE ELEPHANT FIRST!
YOU'RE RIGHT. I'LL CREATE A DIVERSION.
FOX? STOP! IT'S TOO DANGEROUS!
LET HIM BE, LITTLE PRINCE. HE HAS TO DO THIS.
THIS WAY, YOU FILTHY VERMIN! ARE YOU CHICKEN?
NYARGH NYARGH NYARGH!

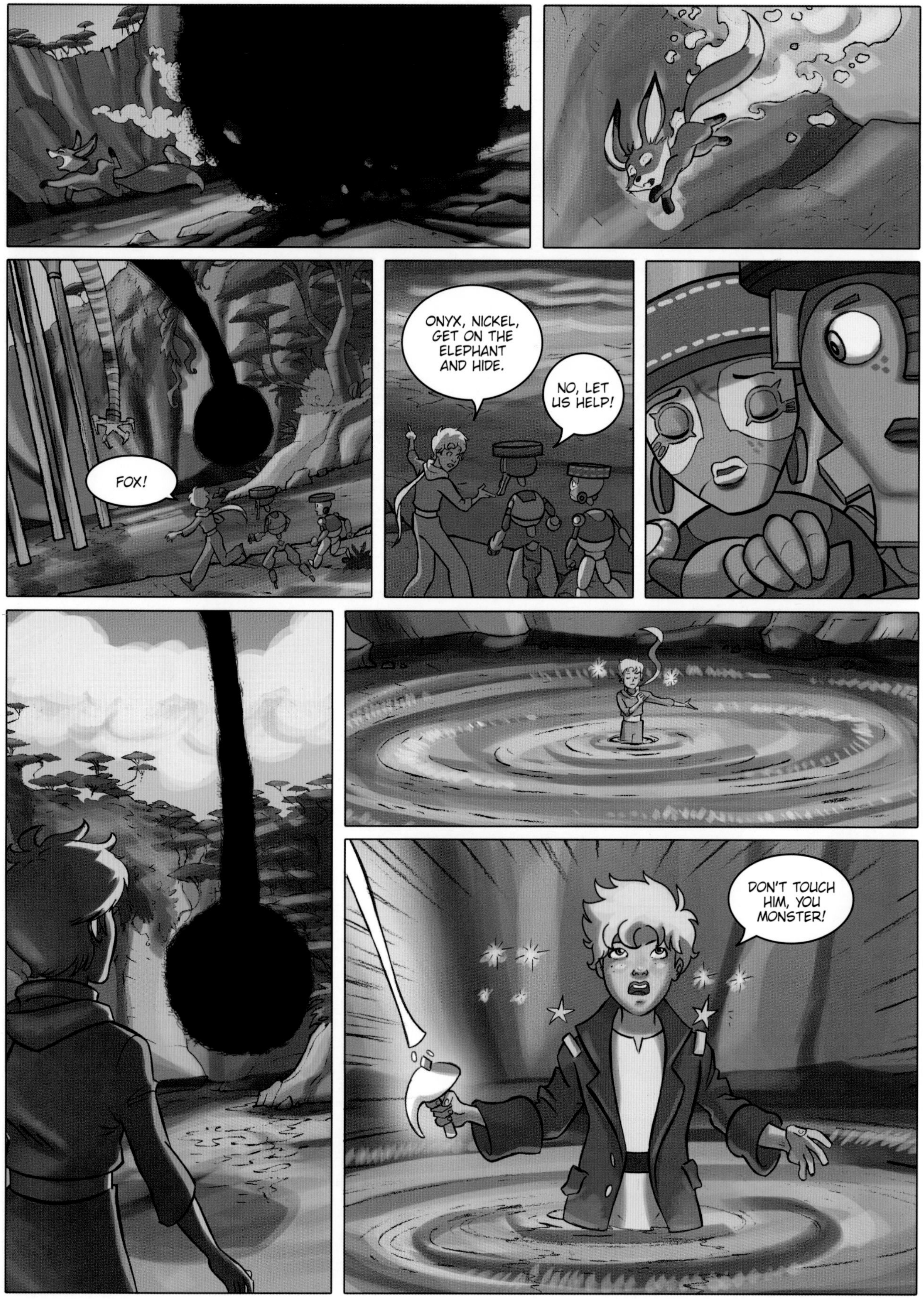
FOX!
ONYX, NICKEL, GET ON THE ELEPHANT AND HIDE.
NO, LET US HELP!
DON'T TOUCH HIM, YOU MONSTER!

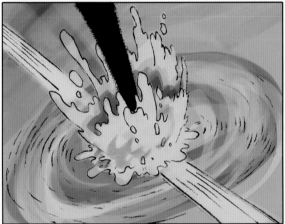

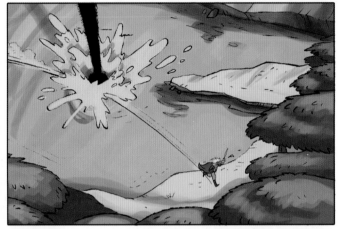

FORGIVE ME, FOX. I SHOULD HAVE BEEN THERE WITH YOU.

THIS WAY, GLOOMIES! I'M THE ONE YOU WANT, RIGHT?

ALMOST THERE...

YOUR TURN, FRIENDS. I CAN'T DO IT ALONE!

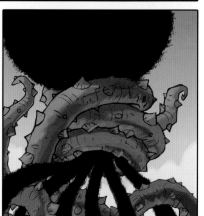

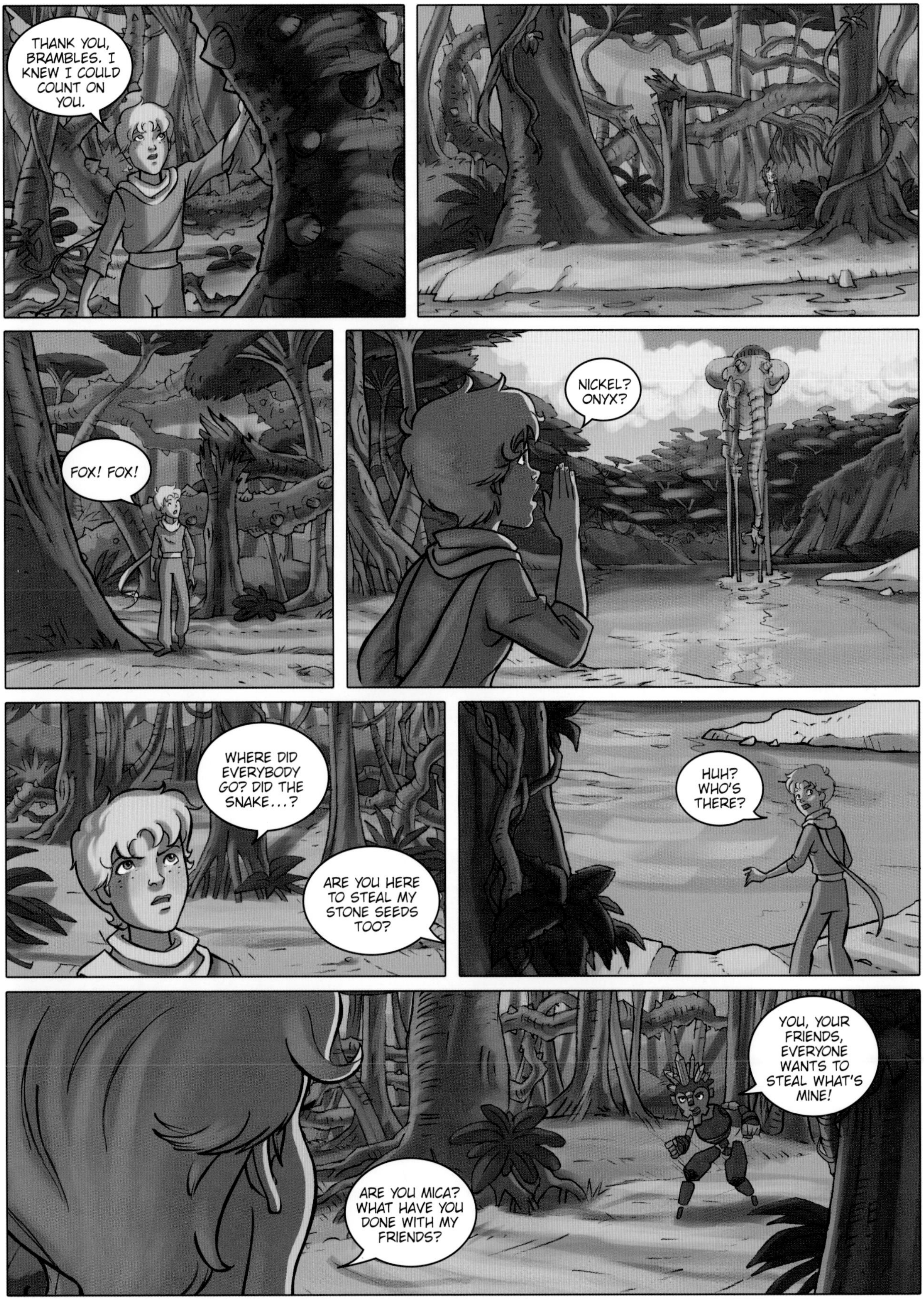
THANK YOU, BRAMBLES. I KNEW I COULD COUNT ON YOU.
FOX! FOX!
NICKEL? ONYX?
WHERE DID EVERYBODY GO? DID THE SNAKE...?
ARE YOU HERE TO STEAL MY STONE SEEDS TOO?
HUH? WHO'S THERE?
ARE YOU MICA? WHAT HAVE YOU DONE WITH MY FRIENDS?
YOU, YOUR FRIENDS, EVERYONE WANTS TO STEAL WHAT'S MINE!

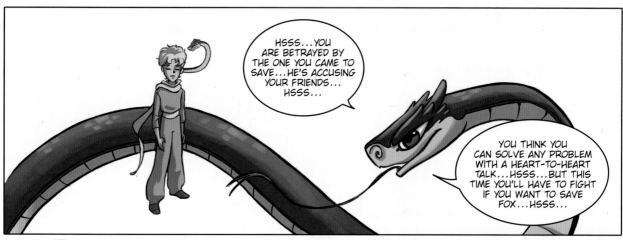

HSSS...YOU ARE BETRAYED BY THE ONE YOU CAME TO SAVE...HE'S ACCUSING YOUR FRIENDS... HSSS...

YOU THINK YOU CAN SOLVE ANY PROBLEM WITH A HEART-TO-HEART TALK...HSSS...BUT THIS TIME YOU'LL HAVE TO FIGHT IF YOU WANT TO SAVE FOX...HSSS...

YOU CAN DO IT! FORCE MICA TO TELL YOU WHAT HE'S DONE WITH YOUR FRIEND...

NO! I WOULD BE NO BETTER THAN YOU IF I ACTED THAT WAY...I WOULD NO LONGER BE WORTHY OF MY ROSE.

THERE'S ANOTHER WAY...

I AM A SERVANT OF THE SNAKE, WHO SENT ME TO HELP YOU, MICA...

WITH MY HELP, YOU'LL FIND THE STONE SEEDS MORE QUICKLY. I AWAIT YOUR ORDERS.

GRRR...FINE, COME WITH ME, BUT YOU'D BETTER NOT BE LYING!

I'M THE LITTLE PRINCE. ALL I DO IS HELP PEOPLE.

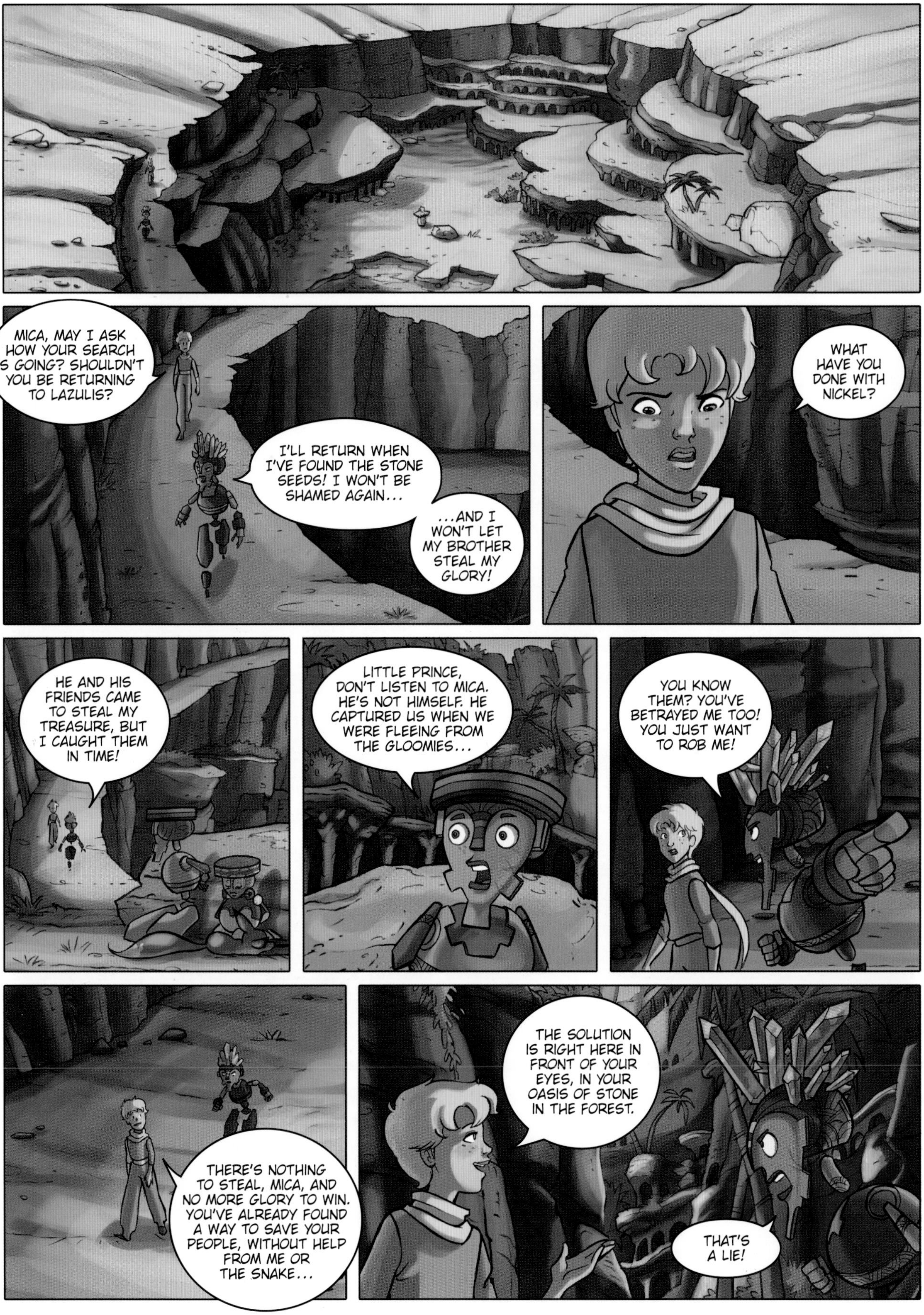
MICA, MAY I ASK HOW YOUR SEARCH IS GOING? SHOULDN'T YOU BE RETURNING TO LAZULIS?
I'LL RETURN WHEN I'VE FOUND THE STONE SEEDS! I WON'T BE SHAMED AGAIN...
...AND I WON'T LET MY BROTHER STEAL MY GLORY!
WHAT HAVE YOU DONE WITH NICKEL?
HE AND HIS FRIENDS CAME TO STEAL MY TREASURE, BUT I CAUGHT THEM IN TIME!
LITTLE PRINCE, DON'T LISTEN TO MICA. HE'S NOT HIMSELF. HE CAPTURED US WHEN WE WERE FLEEING FROM THE GLOOMIES...
YOU KNOW THEM? YOU'VE BETRAYED ME TOO! YOU JUST WANT TO ROB ME!
THERE'S NOTHING TO STEAL, MICA, AND NO MORE GLORY TO WIN. YOU'VE ALREADY FOUND A WAY TO SAVE YOUR PEOPLE, WITHOUT HELP FROM ME OR THE SNAKE...
THE SOLUTION IS RIGHT HERE IN FRONT OF YOUR EYES, IN YOUR OASIS OF STONE IN THE FOREST.
THAT'S A LIE!

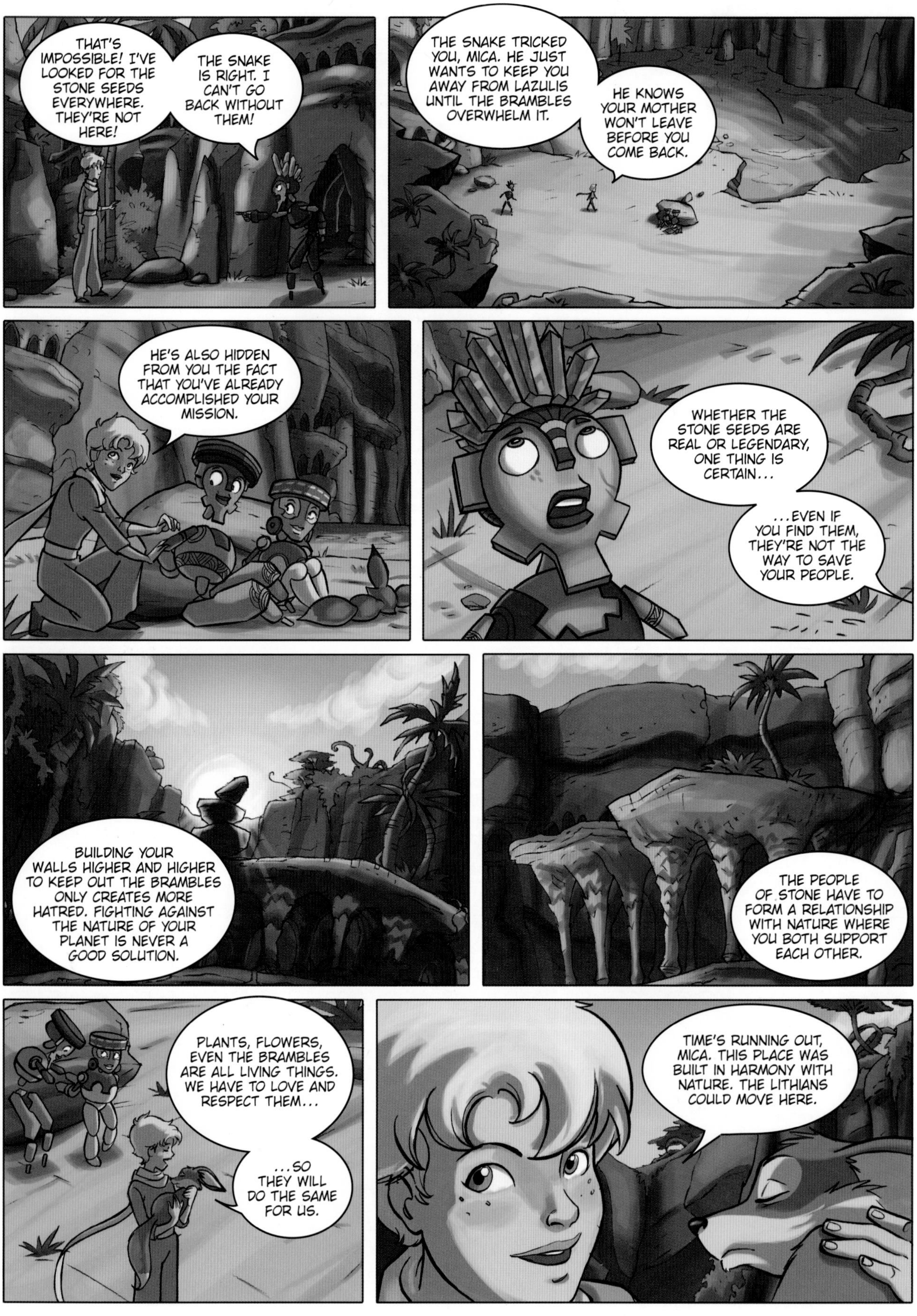
THAT'S IMPOSSIBLE! I'VE LOOKED FOR THE STONE SEEDS EVERYWHERE. THEY'RE NOT HERE!
THE SNAKE IS RIGHT. I CAN'T GO BACK WITHOUT THEM!
THE SNAKE TRICKED YOU, MICA. HE JUST WANTS TO KEEP YOU AWAY FROM LAZULIS UNTIL THE BRAMBLES OVERWHELM IT.
HE KNOWS YOUR MOTHER WON'T LEAVE BEFORE YOU COME BACK.
HE'S ALSO HIDDEN FROM YOU THE FACT THAT YOU'VE ALREADY ACCOMPLISHED YOUR MISSION.
WHETHER THE STONE SEEDS ARE REAL OR LEGENDARY, ONE THING IS CERTAIN...
...EVEN IF YOU FIND THEM, THEY'RE NOT THE WAY TO SAVE YOUR PEOPLE.
BUILDING YOUR WALLS HIGHER AND HIGHER TO KEEP OUT THE BRAMBLES ONLY CREATES MORE HATRED. FIGHTING AGAINST THE NATURE OF YOUR PLANET IS NEVER A GOOD SOLUTION.
THE PEOPLE OF STONE HAVE TO FORM A RELATIONSHIP WITH NATURE WHERE YOU BOTH SUPPORT EACH OTHER.
PLANTS, FLOWERS, EVEN THE BRAMBLES ARE ALL LIVING THINGS. WE HAVE TO LOVE AND RESPECT THEM...
...SO THEY WILL DO THE SAME FOR US.
TIME'S RUNNING OUT, MICA. THIS PLACE WAS BUILT IN HARMONY WITH NATURE. THE LITHIANS COULD MOVE HERE.

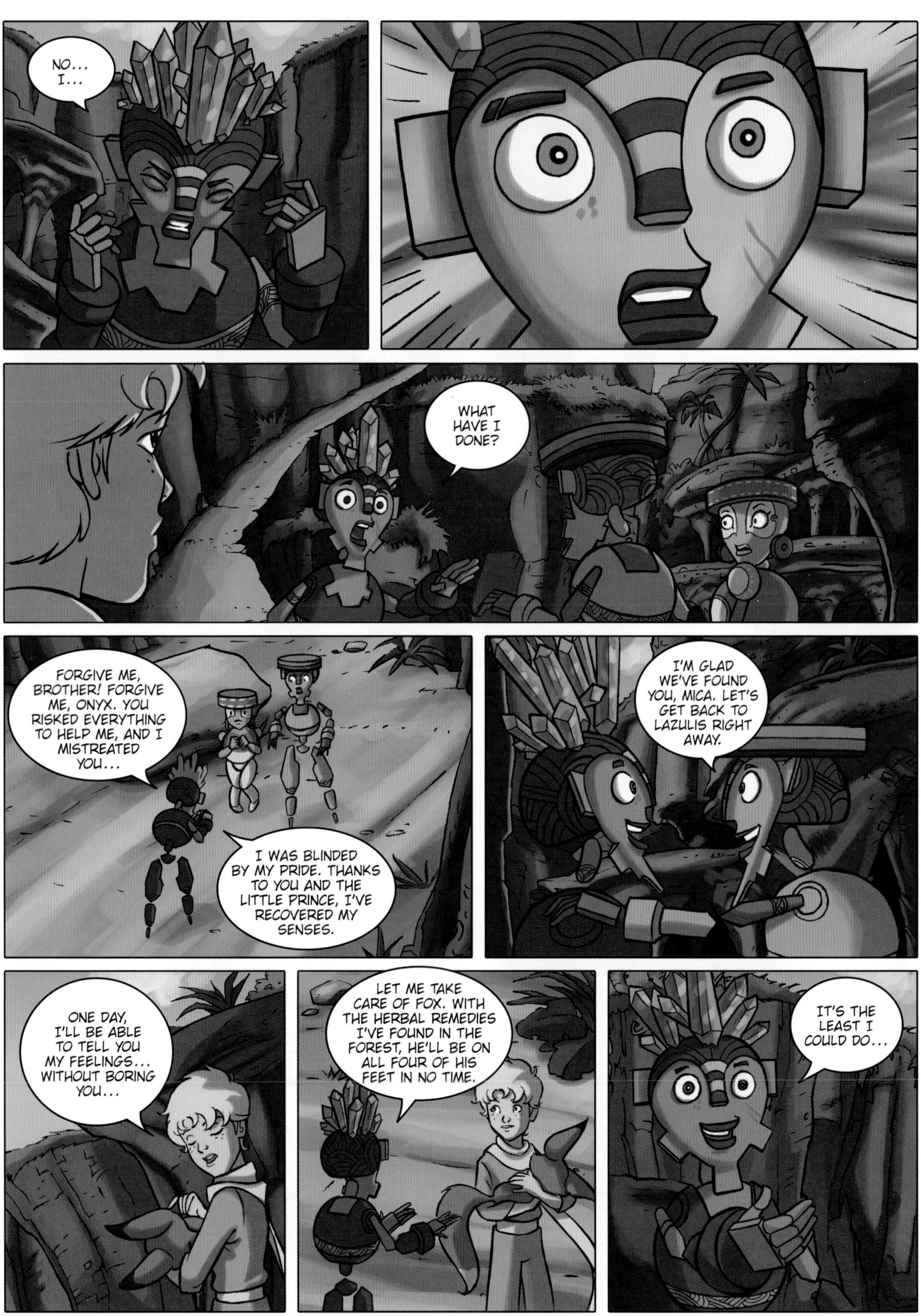
NO... I...
WHAT HAVE I DONE?
FORGIVE ME, BROTHER! FORGIVE ME, ONYX. YOU RISKED EVERYTHING TO HELP ME, AND I MISTREATED YOU...
I WAS BLINDED BY MY PRIDE. THANKS TO YOU AND THE LITTLE PRINCE, I'VE RECOVERED MY SENSES.
I'M GLAD WE'VE FOUND YOU, MICA. LET'S GET BACK TO LAZULIS RIGHT AWAY.
ONE DAY, I'LL BE ABLE TO TELL YOU MY FEELINGS... WITHOUT BORING YOU...
LET ME TAKE CARE OF FOX. WITH THE HERBAL REMEDIES I'VE FOUND IN THE FOREST, HE'LL BE ON ALL FOUR OF HIS FEET IN NO TIME.
IT'S THE LEAST I COULD DO...

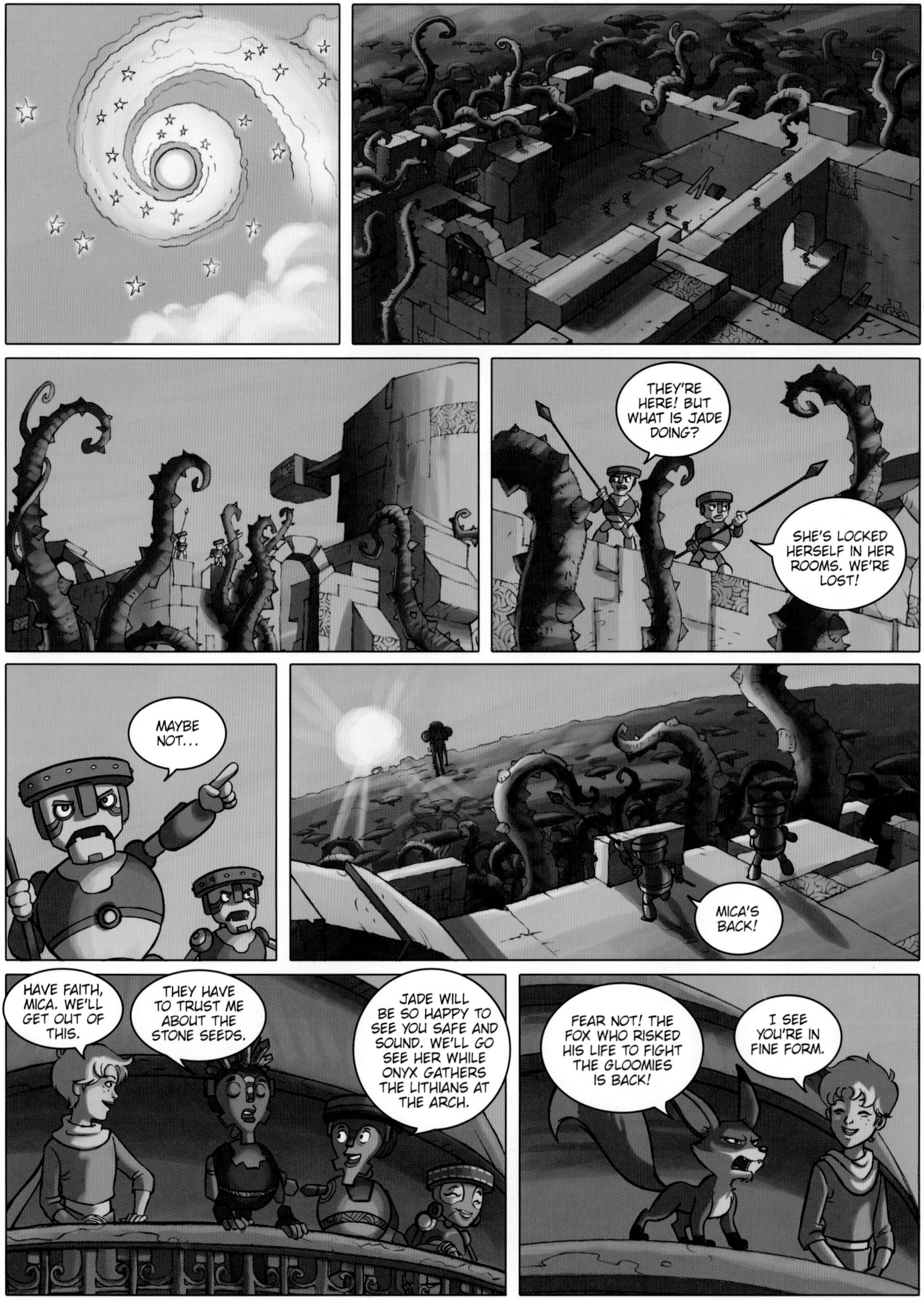
THEY'RE HERE! BUT WHAT IS JADE DOING?
SHE'S LOCKED HERSELF IN HER ROOMS. WE'RE LOST!
MAYBE NOT...
MICA'S BACK!
HAVE FAITH, MICA. WE'LL GET OUT OF THIS.
THEY HAVE TO TRUST ME ABOUT THE STONE SEEDS.
JADE WILL BE SO HAPPY TO SEE YOU SAFE AND SOUND. WE'LL GO SEE HER WHILE ONYX GATHERS THE LITHIANS AT THE ARCH.
FEAR NOT! THE FOX WHO RISKED HIS LIFE TO FIGHT THE GLOOMIES IS BACK!
I SEE YOU'RE IN FINE FORM.

QUEEN JADE, LET US IN! THE BRAMBLES ARE ABOUT TO ATTACK!

IT'S NOT LIKE YOU TO GIVE UP, MOTHER.

MICA?

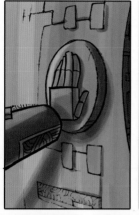

MY SON!

THANK YOU FOR COMING BACK!

QUEEN JADE, TIME IS SHORT. PLEASE ORDER THE EVACUATION OF THE CITY!

THE SOONER THE BETTER!

THERE'S NO NEED. NOW THAT MICA HAS THE STONE SEEDS, WE'RE SAVED!

RIGHT, MICA?

MICA DISCOVERED THAT THE STONE SEEDS ARE ONLY A LEGEND.

HOW CAN THAT BE?

IT'S TRUE! MICA FELL VICTIM TO THE SNAKE, WHO USED MY BROTHER'S DESIRE FOR THE SEEDS TO ENSNARE HIM. BUT MICA FOUND SOMETHING BETTER. HE FOUND A NEW HOME WHERE THE LITHIANS CAN LIVE IN PEACE WITH THE BRAMBLES.

JADE, THE SNAKE WANTS THE PEOPLE OF STONE TO FIGHT THE BRAMBLES, PUTTING YOUR WHOLE WORLD IN PERIL. PLEASE, RETURN THE POWER CRYSTAL FOR THE ARCH SO WE CAN LEAVE.

HSSS... THE LITTLE PRINCE KNOWS YOU STOLE THE CRYSTAL...AND HE'S TRICKED YOUR SON INTO UNDERMINING YOU...HSSS...

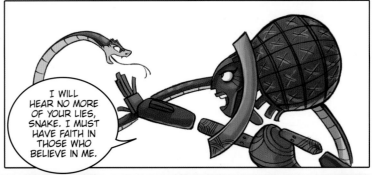

I WILL HEAR NO MORE OF YOUR LIES, SNAKE. I MUST HAVE FAITH IN THOSE WHO BELIEVE IN ME.

MY SONS, I PLACE OUR FATE IN YOUR HANDS.

NICKEL, I WAS THE ONE WHO STOLE YOUR CRYSTAL. I WAS AFRAID YOU'D USE THE ARCH TO RUN AWAY. WILL YOU USE YOUR MACHINE TO GET US ALL OUT OF DANGER?

OF COURSE. COUNT ON ME.

MICA, YOU MUST LEAD US TO A CITY WHERE OUR PEOPLE WILL FIND HAPPINESS...

I WON'T DISAPPOINT YOU, MOTHER.

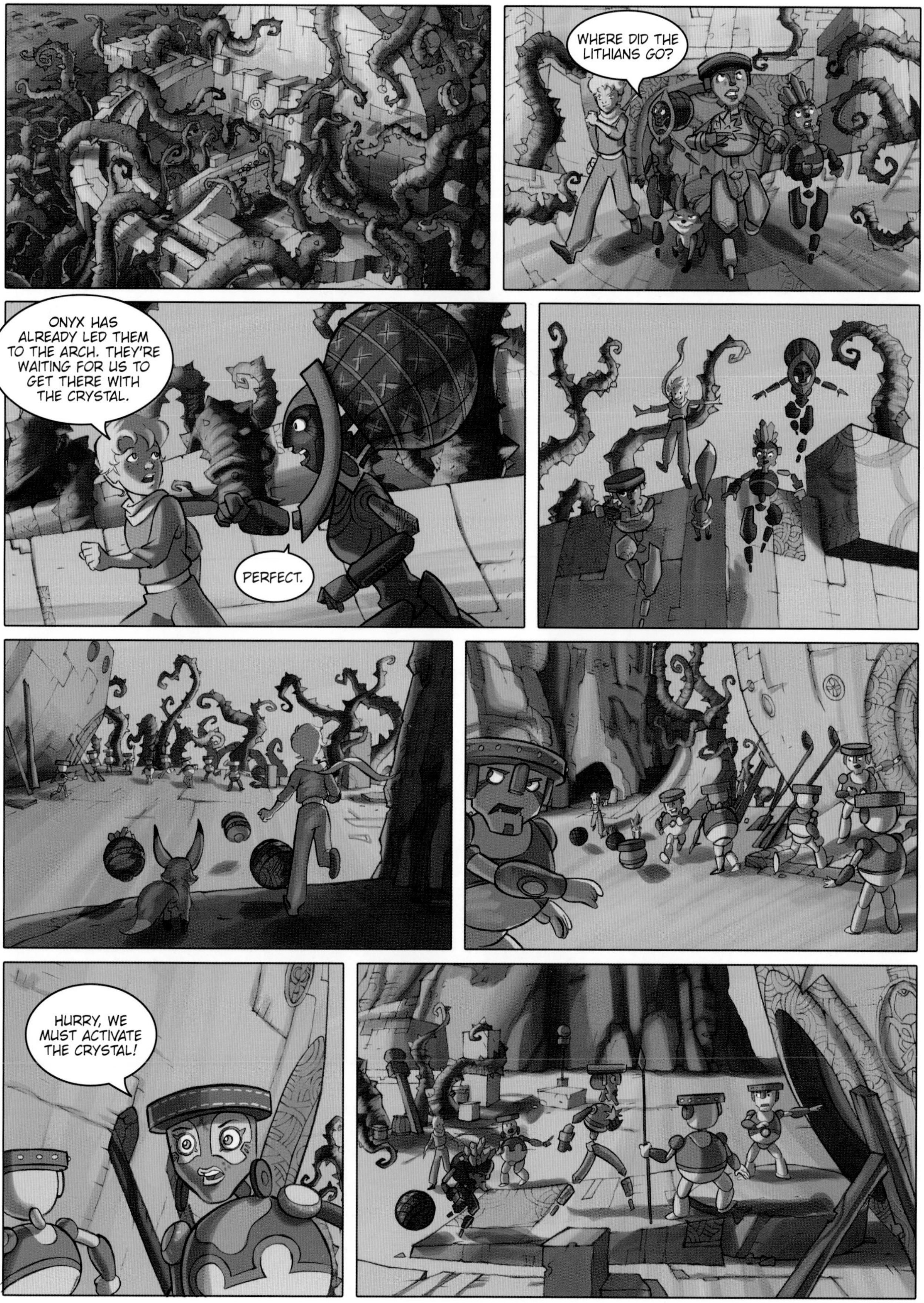
WHERE DID THE LITHIANS GO?
ONYX HAS ALREADY LED THEM TO THE ARCH. THEY'RE WAITING FOR US TO GET THERE WITH THE CRYSTAL.
PERFECT.
HURRY, WE MUST ACTIVATE THE CRYSTAL!

MY DEAR LITHIANS, THANKS TO MICA AND NICKEL, WE WILL SET OUT FOR A PEACEFUL PLACE WHERE YOU CAN LIVE SAFELY.

WE WILL LEARN TO RESPECT NATURE!

I'LL INSTALL THE CRYSTAL, AND NICKEL WILL START UP THE ARCH.

HURRAH!

LONG LIVE JADE!

LET'S GO!

LONG LIVE NICKEL!

LONG LIVE MICA!

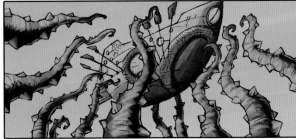

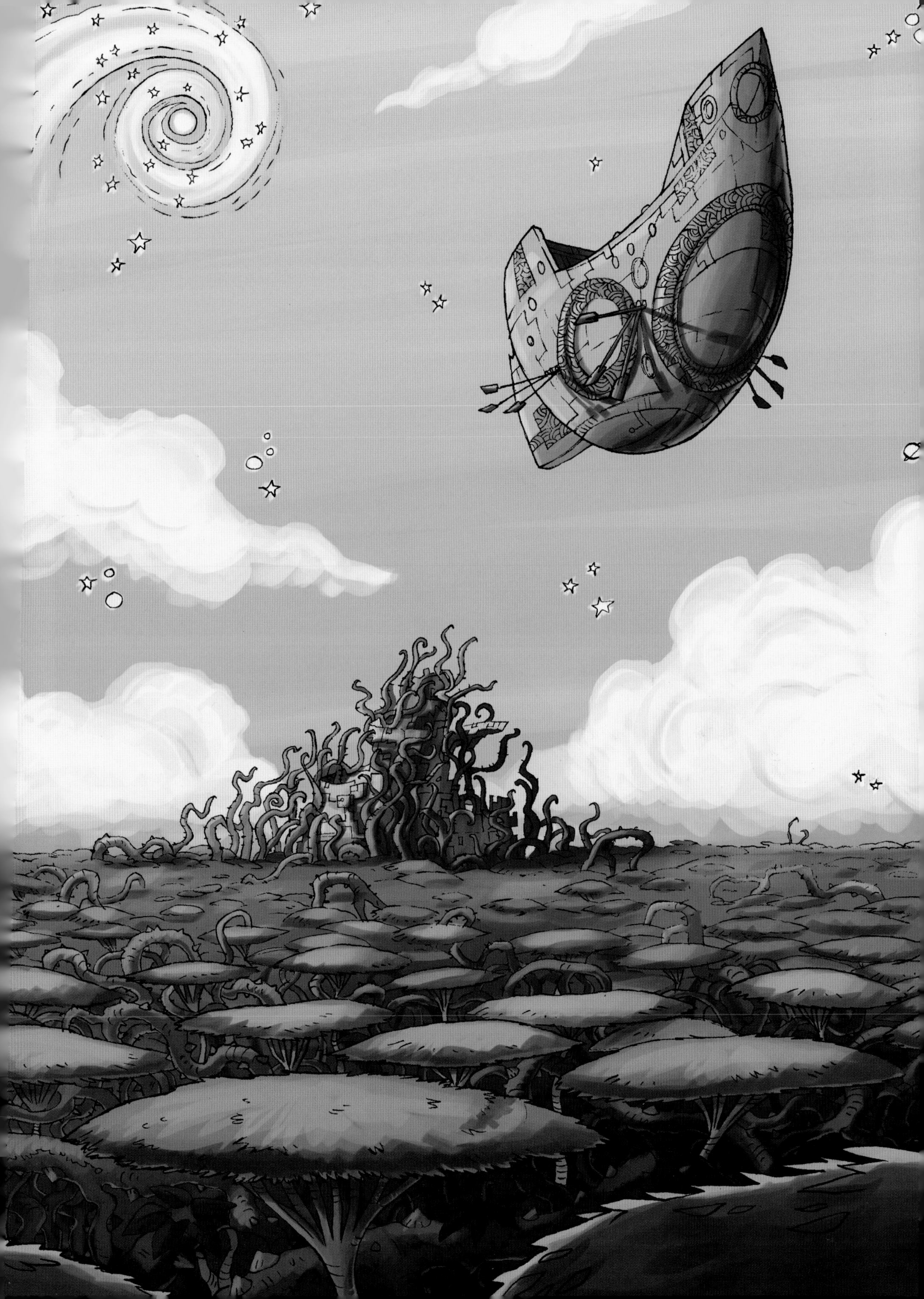

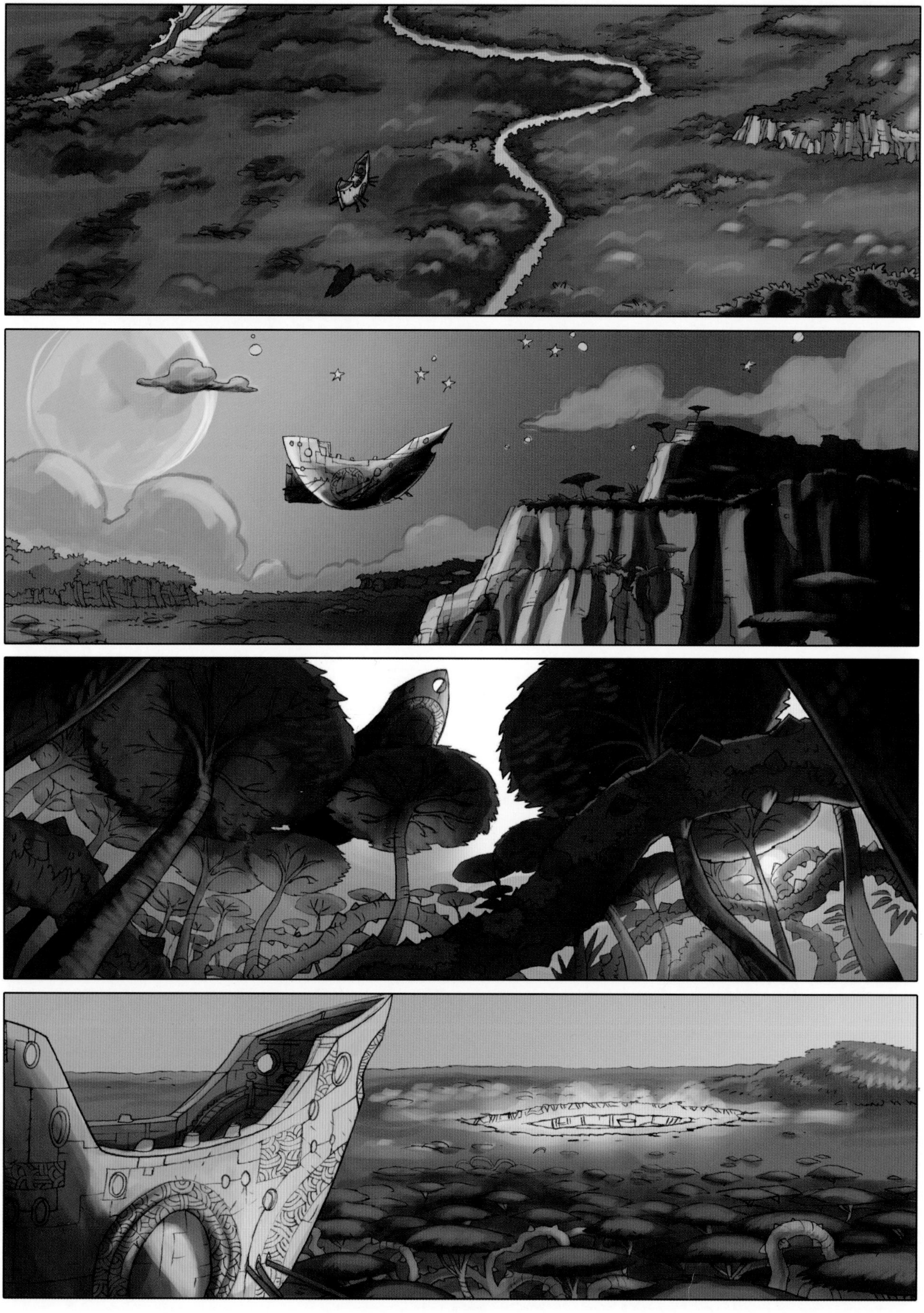

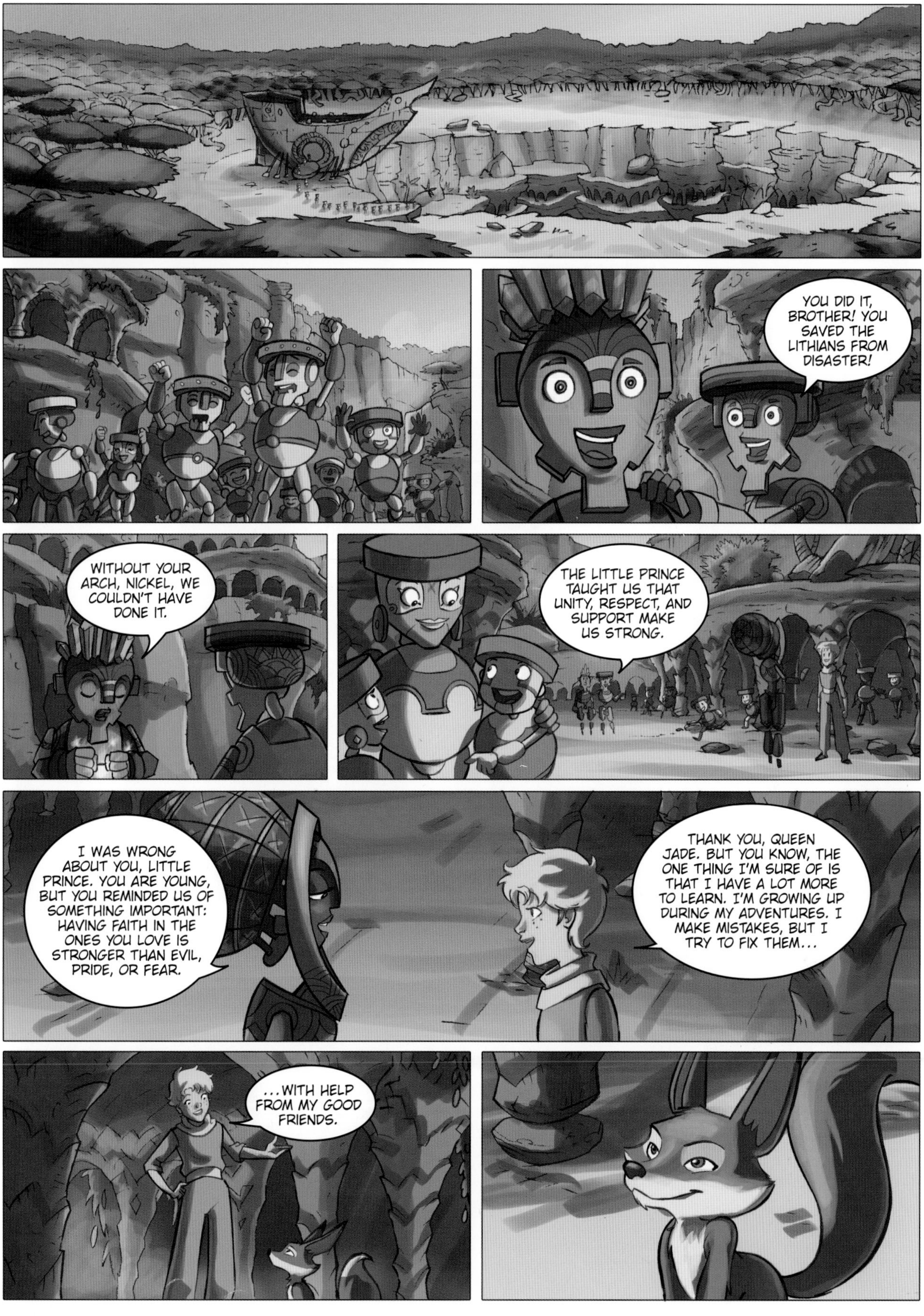
YOU DID IT, BROTHER! YOU SAVED THE LITHIANS FROM DISASTER!
WITHOUT YOUR ARCH, NICKEL, WE COULDN'T HAVE DONE IT.
THE LITTLE PRINCE TAUGHT US THAT UNITY, RESPECT, AND SUPPORT MAKE US STRONG.
I WAS WRONG ABOUT YOU, LITTLE PRINCE. YOU ARE YOUNG, BUT YOU REMINDED US OF SOMETHING IMPORTANT: HAVING FAITH IN THE ONES YOU LOVE IS STRONGER THAN EVIL, PRIDE, OR FEAR.
THANK YOU, QUEEN JADE. BUT YOU KNOW, THE ONE THING I'M SURE OF IS THAT I HAVE A LOT MORE TO LEARN. I'M GROWING UP DURING MY ADVENTURES. I MAKE MISTAKES, BUT I TRY TO FIX THEM...
...WITH HELP FROM MY GOOD FRIENDS.

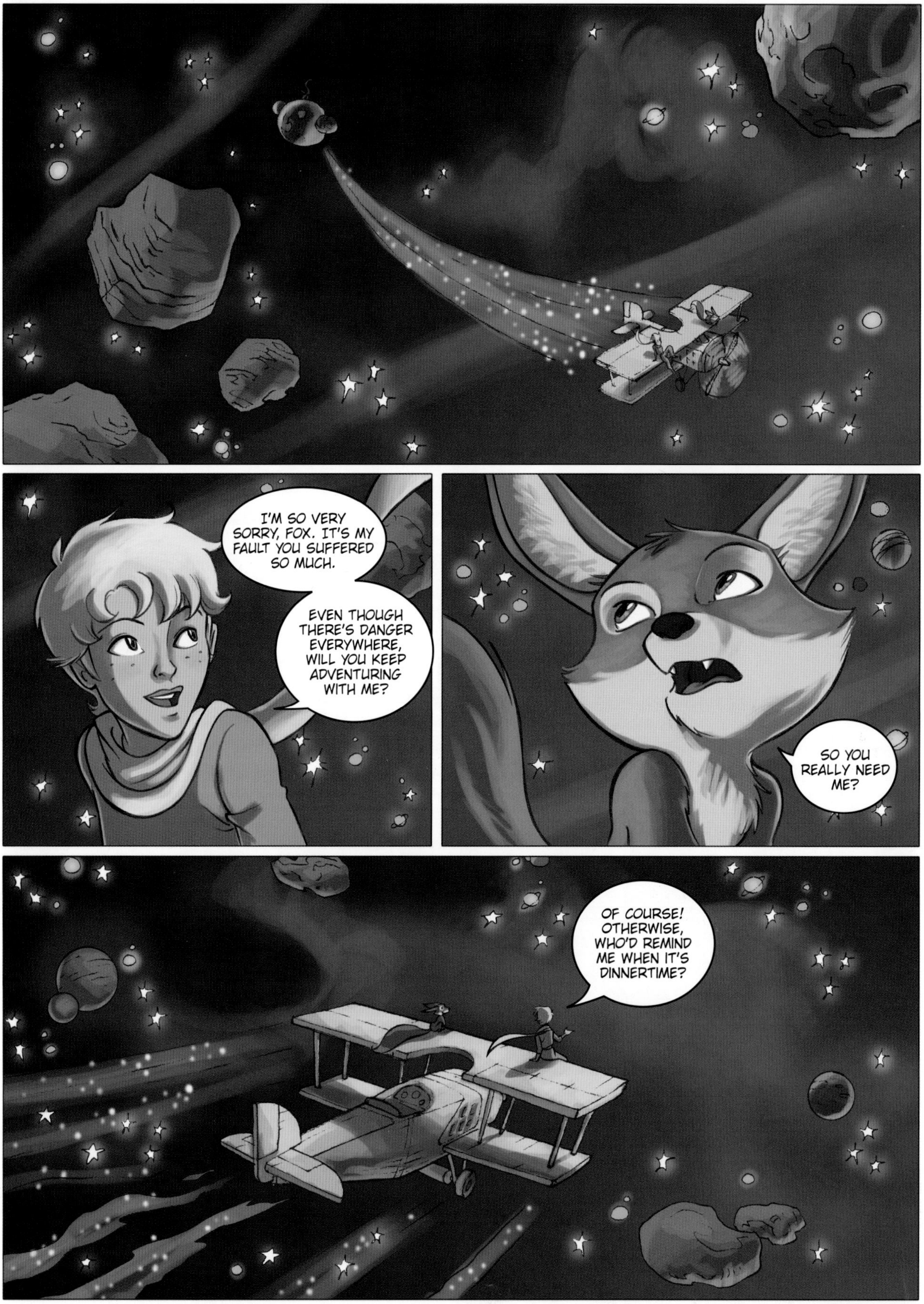
I'M SO VERY SORRY, FOX. IT'S MY FAULT YOU SUFFERED SO MUCH.
EVEN THOUGH THERE'S DANGER EVERYWHERE, WILL YOU KEEP ADVENTURING WITH ME?
SO YOU REALLY NEED ME?
OF COURSE! OTHERWISE, WHO'D REMIND ME WHEN IT'S DINNERTIME?

THE END

The Little Prince

AS IMAGINED BY

MATTHIEU
BONHOMME

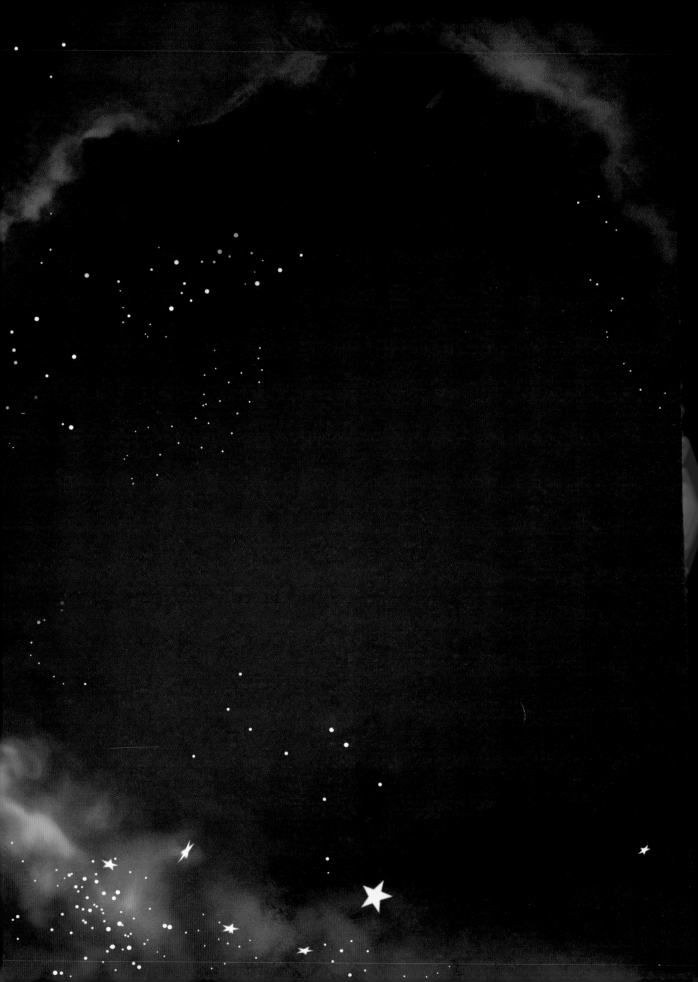

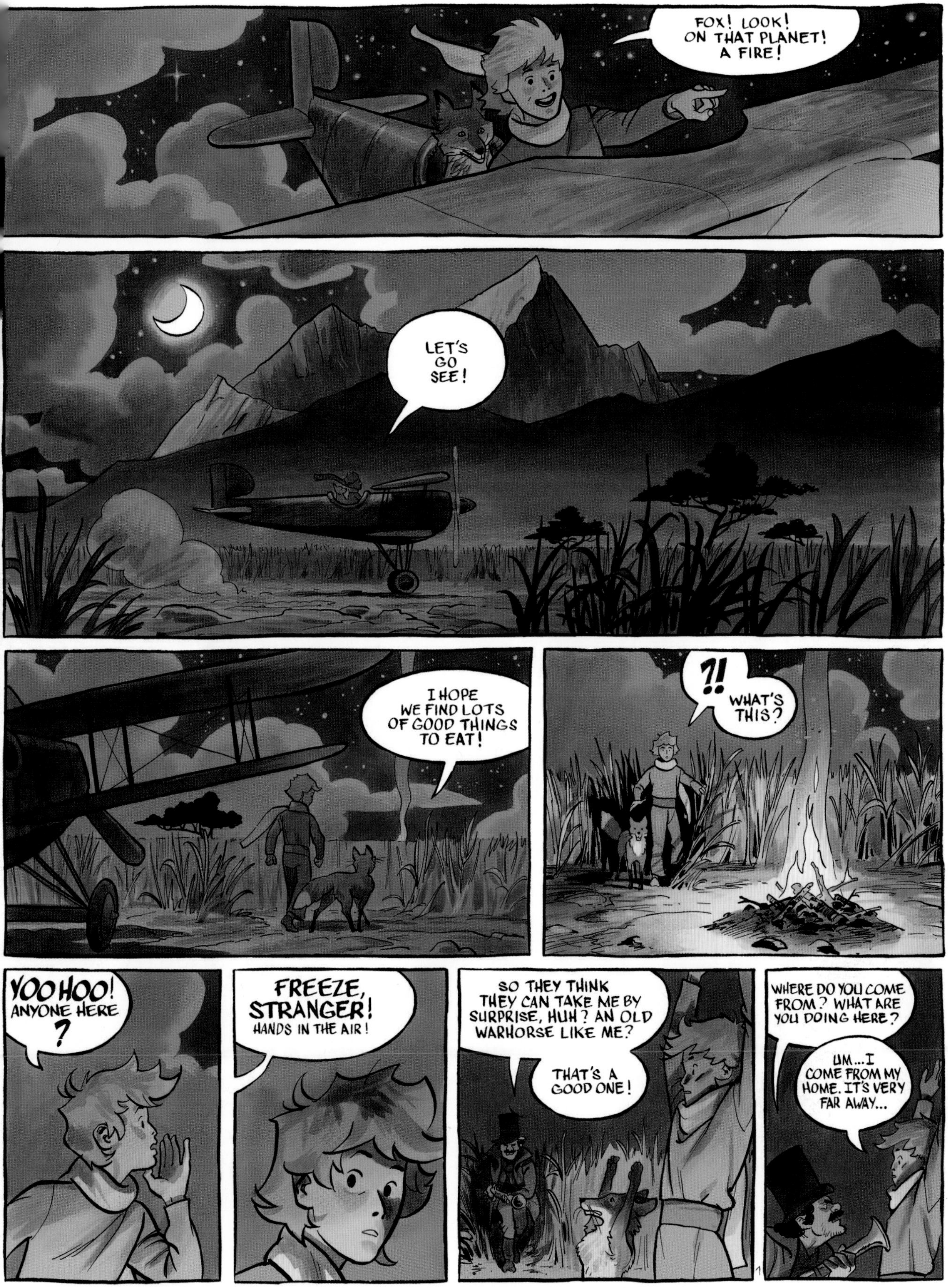
FOX! LOOK! ON THAT PLANET! A FIRE!
LET'S GO SEE!
I HOPE WE FIND LOTS OF GOOD THINGS TO EAT!
?!! WHAT'S THIS?
YOO HOO! ANYONE HERE ?
FREEZE, STRANGER! HANDS IN THE AIR!
SO THEY THINK THEY CAN TAKE ME BY SURPRISE, HUH? AN OLD WARHORSE LIKE ME?
THAT'S A GOOD ONE!
WHERE DO YOU COME FROM? WHAT ARE YOU DOING HERE?
UM...I COME FROM MY HOME. IT'S VERY FAR AWAY...

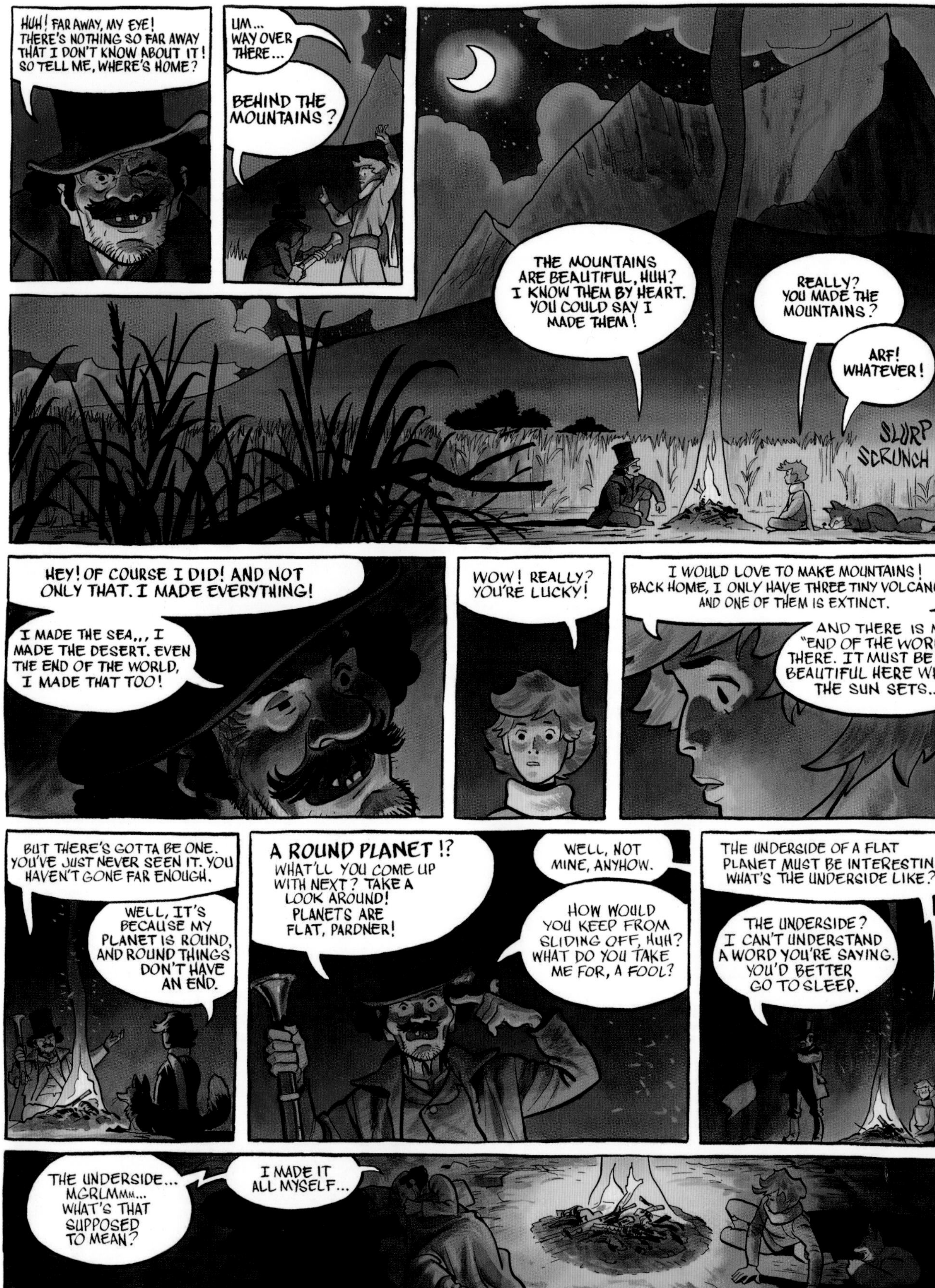
HUH! FAR AWAY, MY EYE! THERE'S NOTHING SO FAR AWAY THAT I DON'T KNOW ABOUT IT! SO TELL ME, WHERE'S HOME?
UM... WAY OVER THERE...
BEHIND THE MOUNTAINS?
THE MOUNTAINS ARE BEAUTIFUL, HUH? I KNOW THEM BY HEART. YOU COULD SAY I MADE THEM!
REALLY? YOU MADE THE MOUNTAINS?
ARF! WHATEVER!
SLURP
SCRUNCH
HEY! OF COURSE I DID! AND NOT ONLY THAT. I MADE EVERYTHING!
I MADE THE SEA,,, I MADE THE DESERT. EVEN THE END OF THE WORLD, I MADE THAT TOO!
WOW! REALLY? YOU'RE LUCKY!
I WOULD LOVE TO MAKE MOUNTAINS! BACK HOME, I ONLY HAVE THREE TINY VOLCANOES, AND ONE OF THEM IS EXTINCT.
AND THERE IS NO "END OF THE WORLD" THERE. IT MUST BE SO BEAUTIFUL HERE WHEN THE SUN SETS...
BUT THERE'S GOTTA BE ONE. YOU'VE JUST NEVER SEEN IT. YOU HAVEN'T GONE FAR ENOUGH.
WELL, IT'S BECAUSE MY PLANET IS ROUND, AND ROUND THINGS DON'T HAVE AN END.
A ROUND PLANET!? WHAT'LL YOU COME UP WITH NEXT? TAKE A LOOK AROUND! PLANETS ARE FLAT, PARDNER!
WELL, NOT MINE, ANYHOW.
HOW WOULD YOU KEEP FROM SLIDING OFF, HUH? WHAT DO YOU TAKE ME FOR, A FOOL?
THE UNDERSIDE OF A FLAT PLANET MUST BE INTERESTING. WHAT'S THE UNDERSIDE LIKE?
THE UNDERSIDE? I CAN'T UNDERSTAND A WORD YOU'RE SAYING. YOU'D BETTER GO TO SLEEP.
THE UNDERSIDE... MGRLMmm... WHAT'S THAT SUPPOSED TO MEAN?
I MADE IT ALL MYSELF...

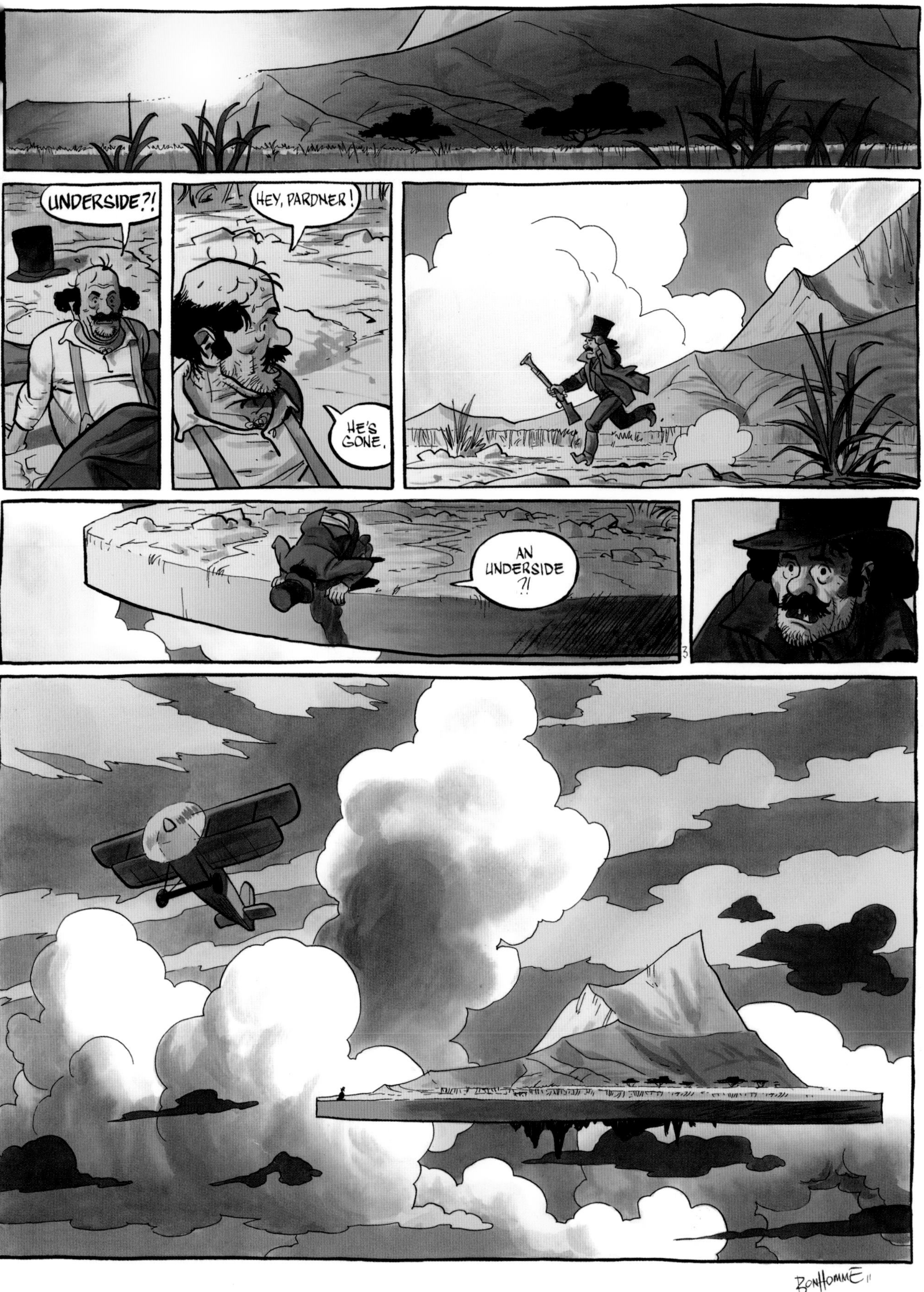
UNDERSIDE?!
HEY, PARDNER!
HE'S GONE.
AN UNDERSIDE ?!
BONHOMME 11

Antoine de Saint-Exupéry
Aviator • Author • Adventurer • Hero

Antoine de Saint-Exupéry, author of the novel *The Little Prince* on which these new adventures are based, was born on June 29, 1900, in Lyon, France. He was the third of five children: Marie-Madeleine, Simone, Antoine, François, and Gabrielle. It was when he was twelve years old, during his summer break from boarding school, that airplanes and flying first made a huge impression on him.

In 1920, he was accepted into the École des Beaux-Arts in Paris to study architecture, but the next year he joined the Second Aviation Regiment of the armed forces and received his pilot's license. In 1922, he had his first plane crash and suffered a head fracture. He had to leave the armed forces and work at different jobs on the ground to earn a living.

By May of 1926, Saint-Exupéry was able to fly again. He delivered airmail, which was a new and sometimes dangerous profession, on routes from France to Senegal and all the way to South America. That was where, in 1931, he met and married Consuelo Suncin.

From 1933 to 1938, Saint-Exupéry was very busy. He traveled to North Africa and Indochina and attempted to break the flight speed record from Paris to Saigon, Vietnam—during which his plane crashed again. It went down in the middle of the Sahara Desert. After his recovery, his life became even busier. He wrote newspaper reports in Spain on the Spanish Civil War, scouted airplane routes between Casablanca and Timbuktu, wrote a screenplay, registered several patents, and traveled to the United States. In 1939, with the start of World War II, he returned to France and talked his way into a job as a high-risk reconnaissance pilot for the French Air Force. But this only lasted until France reached an armistice agreement with Germany.

In December 1940, Saint-Exupéry returned to visit friends in New York, where he finally began work on *The Little Prince.* The story is narrated by a pilot who has crashed his plane into the Sahara Desert. He meets a little prince visiting from a faraway asteroid. Along the way, the prince also meets Fox and Snake. By late 1942, after spending the spring and summer writing and illustrating, Saint-Exupéry had completed his novel, and in April 1943 it was published in his native language of French *(Le Petit Prince)* and in English.

Saint-Exupéry was eager to return to the war. He decided to join the Free French Forces in Algeria, who were continuing the fight against the Axis powers. Because of his age, at first he had a hard time convincing them to let him fly. He was authorized to fly five dangerous missions. In fact, he flew eight. On July 31, 1944, Saint-Exupéry went on a scouting flight to prepare for military landings in the south of France. His plane disappeared over the water, and he was never seen again.

Over the decades since *The Little Prince* was published, it has gone on to become one of the best-selling novels of all time. In 2003, a small moon in our solar system's asteroid belt was named Petit-Prince in honor of the masterpiece Saint-Exupéry created.

THE LITTLE PRINCE IN THE TWENTY-FIRST CENTURY

The Little Prince is a landmark of literature and one of the most translated and beloved books in the world. It tackles universal topics with a unique philosophical and poetic sensibility. Sixty-five years after the first edition, the Saint-Exupéry Estate decided to bring the character back for a whole new generation . . . and for everyone who has ever loved the boy who sees the world with his heart.

The Little Prince now returns in a series of new adventures that remain true to the spirit of the original work. He will travel from planet to planet chasing the wicked Snake, who wants to plunge the whole universe into darkness. On each planet, the Snake sends bad thoughts into the minds of its inhabitants, making them sad and grim, draining the life out of their planet. The Little Prince must leave his beautiful Rose behind and must use his vision and courage to defeat the Snake, bringing along his friend Fox to save planets in danger across the universe.

ABOUT THE ADAPTERS

After several years in video games and Japanese animation, adapter Guillaume Dorison became literary editor for the publisher Les Humanoïdes Associés in 2006, where he launched the Shogun Collection dedicated to original manga. In June 2010, he founded Élyum Studio with Didier Poli, Jean-Baptiste Hostache, and Xavier Dorison to provide services for the creation of graphic novels. In addition to his position as director of writing for Élyum Studio, he has more than two dozen comics and manga to his credit under the pseudonym IZU, has written several titles in the Explora series on world explorers for French publisher Glénat, and won the 2010 Animeland Prize for best French manga.

Didier Poli, artistic director for the new graphic novel adaptations based on *The Little Prince*, was born in Lyon in 1971. After graduate studies in applied arts, he worked for various animation studios including Disney. He was working as artistic director for the video game company Kalisto Entertainment when he met Manuel Bichebois in 2001 and began drawing Bichebois' graphic novel series L'Enfant de l'orage. At the 2004 Nîmes Festival, Didier Poli received the Bronze Boar prize for young talent. He continues, along with his work on graphic novels, to work regularly in cartoons and video games as a designer and storyboard artist.

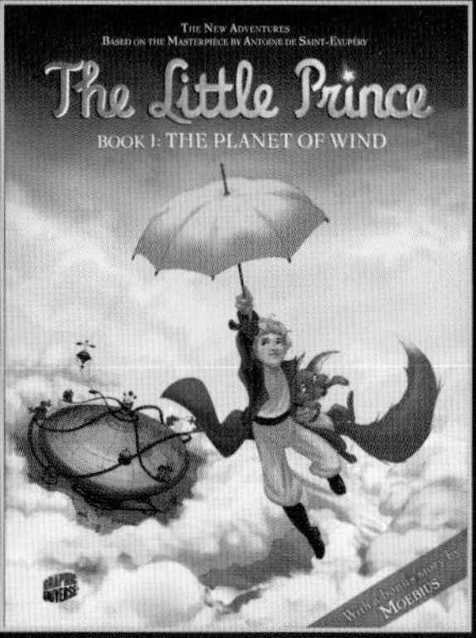
The New Adventures
Based on the Masterpiece by Antoine de Saint-Exupéry
The Little Prince
BOOK 1: THE PLANET OF WIND
MOEBIUS

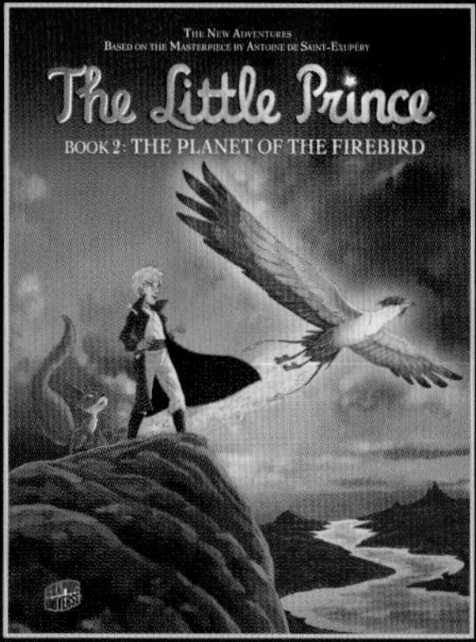
The New Adventures
Based on the Masterpiece by Antoine de Saint-Exupéry
The Little Prince
BOOK 2: THE PLANET OF THE FIREBIRD

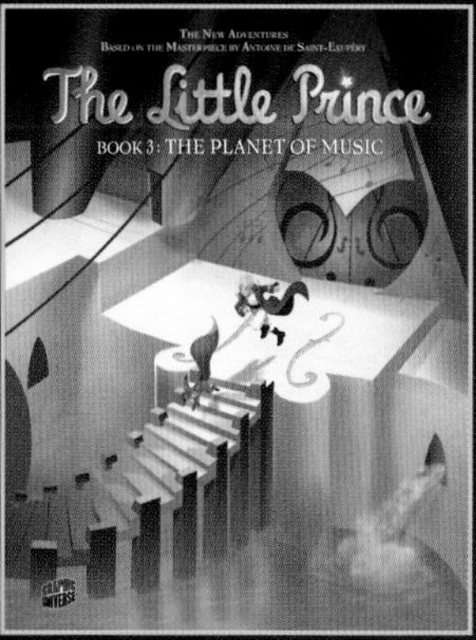
The New Adventures
Based on the Masterpiece by Antoine de Saint-Exupéry
The Little Prince
BOOK 3: THE PLANET OF MUSIC

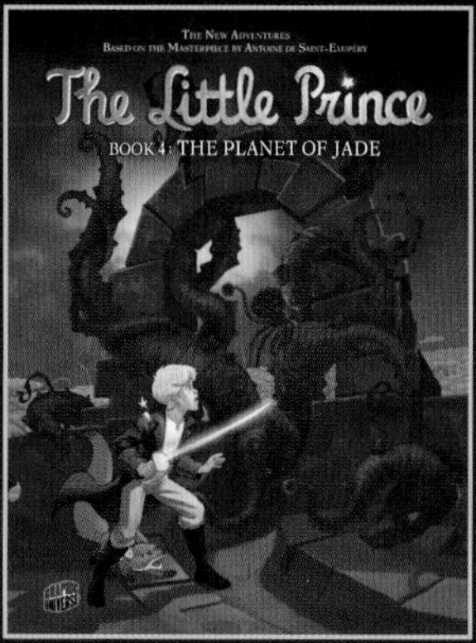
The New Adventures
Based on the Masterpiece by Antoine de Saint-Exupéry
The Little Prince
BOOK 4: THE PLANET OF JADE

Book 1: The Planet of Wind

Book 2: The Planet of the Firebird

Book 3: The Planet of Music

Book 4: The Planet of Jade

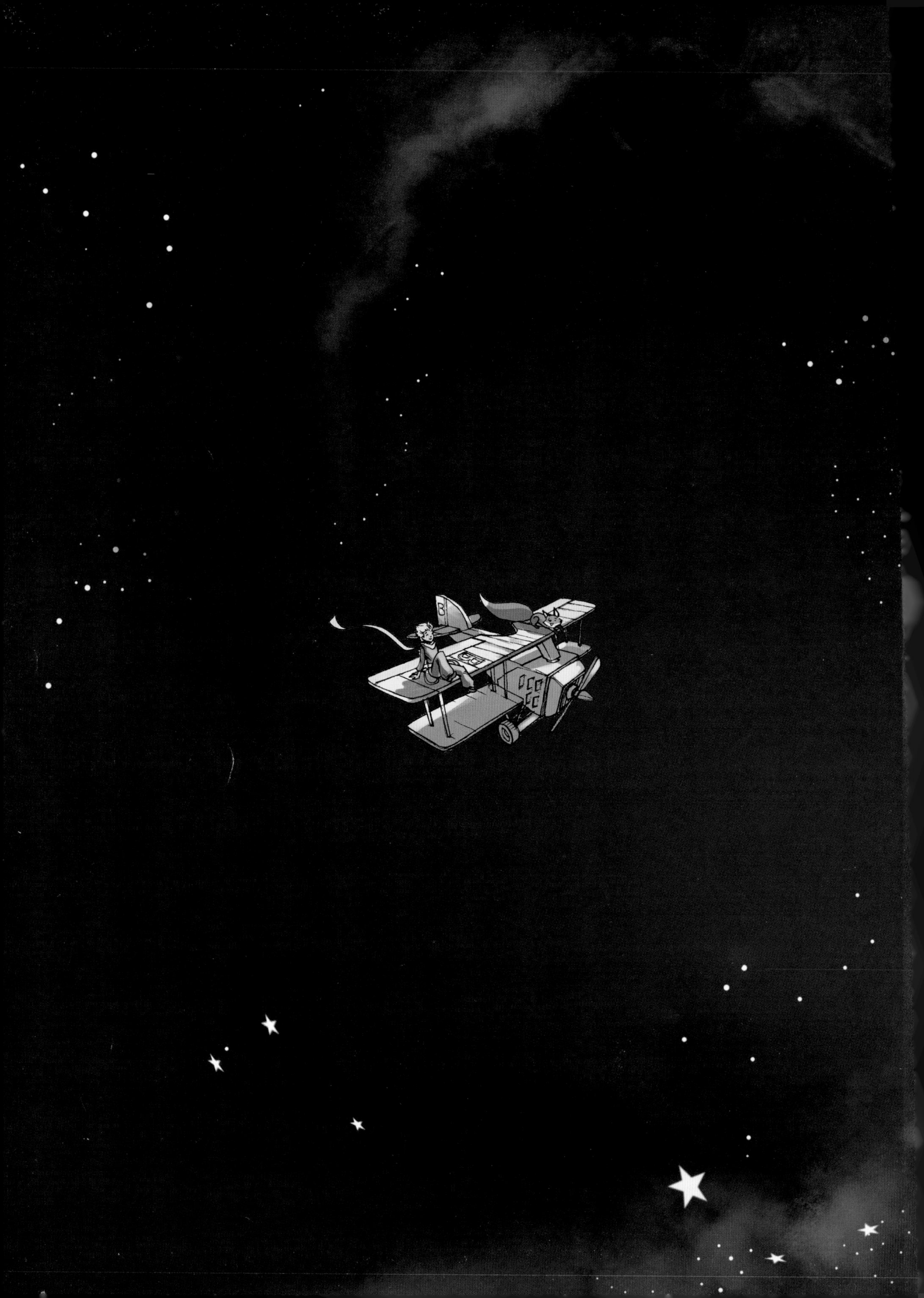